Short Stories

from India, Pakistan and Bangladesh

Short Stories

from India, Pakistan and Bangladesh

Ranjana

Harrap  **London**

First published in Great Britain 1980
by HARRAP LIMITED
19–23 Ludgate Hill, London EC4M 7PD

Reprinted: 1982

ISBN 0 245-53571-3

Cover photograph—Margaret Murray

Printed and bound in Great Britain by
Robert Hartnoll Ltd. Bodmin, Cornwall

Contents

Introduction

The main aim of this anthology is to introduce students in secondary schools and colleges of further education to the literature of the subcontinent of India, Pakistan and Bangladesh. While it is hoped that the book will prove interesting to students and teachers irrespective of their cultural background, the presence in British educational institutions of students from South Asia makes its purpose more relevant. Many of the descendants of immigrants, born and brought up in Britain, are either quite ignorant of the heritage rooted in their parents' land or very parochial in their knowledge and outlook. Growing up in a ghetto in a British city with others from their part of the subcontinent, they do not know or appreciate the diversity of cultures, languages, literature and life-styles in that part of the world.

For too long the literature of the subcontinent has been ignored in the West and even those professing an interest have too often been preoccupied with authors who write in English. But Indo-Anglian writers, like Mulk Raj Anand or R. K. Narayan form a tiny proportion of the large number of writers who choose to express themselves in their mother tongue. This is not the place to dwell on the long, literary history of these lands. Those interested can turn to the standard texts giving in the reading list at the end of this introduction. An anthology, selected from short stories written in the regional languages, should prove a convenient entry into the literature of India, Pakistan and Bangladesh.

The use of literature to understand a foreign culture has only recently been appreciated. The external facts and figures provided by the social sciences and other academic disciplines need to be balanced by an inner view—the way in which the people within the culture view it. The combination of aesthetic sensibility and distance that a good writer possesses should prove a valuable approach to multicultural understanding. This anthology, it is hoped, will prove useful to the teacher discussing India's rural stratification or the changing life-style of Pakistani women as well as to the English teacher trying to widen the range of literary experiences of his/her class.

India has always been a great treasury of tales—folk, classical, romantic, fantastic, moralistic. Stories from the *Panchatantra* found their way into many lands while the story-cycle in which the same character had innumerable adventures became a useful literary device. Later on, there were stories of romance and fantasy to provide escape. But the serious story with its unity of theme and tone and compressed statement of life is a relatively recent phenomenon. In India, the influence of European masters like Maupassant, Turgenev and Chekhov came through translations. Tagore, for instance, read them through his brother's translations and was influenced by them. He, in turn, influenced writers in different parts of the country so that by the time the First World War ended and the struggle for national independence had been taken to new levels by Gandhi, the short story had become well established.

Right from the start, its greatest exponents, from Tagore to Premchand, Tarashankar, Manik Bandopadhyay and the left-wing writers of the thirties and forties, saw the short story as social comment. Even where the writers were not particularly committed to social reform, the approach was naturalistic rather than didactic.

It was not until the fifties that a different kind of short story began to appear. Called the 'new story', it dealt with the private world of alienated and divided young men and women who were not as concerned with social causes and themes as were their predecessors. Sexual freedom, a turning away from traditional morality, loneliness—these are the themes of the 'new' writers. But even they cannot forget the realities of life in the subcontinent today—highly politicised and constantly erupting into conflict between rival classes, castes and political parties. There have been three wars between India and Pakistan since 1947—the last over the creation of Bangladesh. Writers, unless they are very determined to escape, cannot avoid their social milieu. The two stories by Kamleshwar and Gangopadhyay are full of social comment.

If there seems to be a preponderance of stories with a rural setting, it is only natural. The great majority of the people in all three countries live in villages, and farming continues to be the single, most important occupation. But there is another reason for the rural bias. It is to provide students, often growing up in the inner city areas of Britain, with some idea of the way of life and the values and hopes of the peasants in what is now called the Third World. Their poverty and exploitation receive superficial publicity but their own view of life—their role as the makers of culture—is a closed book. Attitudes of patronising benevolence or outright contempt can only be rectified by seeing poverty and suffering through the eyes of a master like Premchand. Halku in *January Night* is a poor tenant farmer who loses his land to join the ranks of landless agricultural labourers. Tarini is a penniless boatman determined to survive the flood that drowns his wife and smashes his boat. But not all peasants live on the verge of starvation. Qasmi's rural families, like those of Hazara Singh in Virk's story, are well-to-do but their life-style and values are quite distinct from those of urbanised people.

The period covered in these stories was dominated by the struggle for independence from British rule. Nationalism therefore plays a prominent part, both from the point of view of the ardent patriot like Manto's tonga driver in *The New Constitution* and the person who identifies with his rulers, like the arrogant aristocrat in Pannalal Patel's *The Jagirdar and his Dog*. But the struggle for independence came about through the division of the country caused by the Partition of August 1947. Partition meant that parts of the country where the majority of the population was Muslim, namely East Bengal, West Punjab, Sindh and the North-west Frontier Province were detached from the rest of India to become Pakistan. This division had been preceded by riots between the different communities and savage killing, looting and rape continued after Partition with religious fanaticism being stirred up by politicians for their own ends. The Partition saw the transfer of whole populations from one state to another. This mass migration of refugees is termed the subcontinent's holocaust and it involved the displacement of millions of people together with the loss of their property. The newly independent states of India and Pakistan were faced with rehabilitation of destitute people who might previously have enjoyed economic security and affluence.

One of the saddest aspects of the transfer of people from one side of the border to the other was the fate of those women who were abducted and forced to live as the wives or concubines of the men who had raped them. Committees for finding these women were set up in both countries and in several instances they were located and brought back to be reunited with their families but often they were not accepted. Their relatives rejectd them because they had been dishonoured and would bring dishonour to the family. To counter such ideas, social reformers tried to change people's hearts and values by means of propaganda. Bedi's story, *Lajwanti,* is one of the finest expressions of the sort of conflict that can arise from such a situation.

The fact of social change in what are simplistically called 'traditional' societies tends to be minimised or misconstrued. The usual desire for immigrants to retain their ethnic identity makes for a failure to keep abreast of the changes that are taking place in their country of origin. The impact of capitalism is to be seen throughout the subcontinent. The segregation of women by means of the veil or otherwise is now on the decline. Likewise, women's education is expanding and they are now able to enter many more professions and occupations than in the past. Taboos and prohibitions are weakening. Qasmi's *Compulsions* is a masterly account of the changes that follow when people have to leave the village and are caught up in what passes for modernisation. Jahangir's story of an unemployed university graduate, *Monsoon,* shows the changes taking place within the family as the son can no longer obey and respect his parents.

The ultimate reality is hunger and three of the stories deal with the need for food and survival at its most elemental level. Shamsuddin's *The Leader* is a mordant account of the hollowness of an alleged leftist politician when confronted with starvation during the Bengal Famine of 1943 which killed millions. Tarashankar's *Tarini, the Boatman* is a study of the determination to live even at the cost of killing one's loved one. Gangopadhyay's *Baby Deer* exposes the selfishness and callousness of educated middle-class tourists when face to face with hungry village children.

The relations between men and women are dealt with in three stories about marriage as seen from different social standpoints. Jainendra's *The Prize* is the typical lower middle-class urban marriage with the jealous and unhappy wife incapable of doing more than grumble and suffer. Tagore's *Appeasement* wittily reveals the typical double standard of morality, ubiquitous at the turn of the century and still prevalent. Amrita Pritam's *The Stench of Kerosene* depicts the tradgedy of a barren wife when her husband is forced to take a second wife to get a son.

The religiosity and fondness for a variety of spiritual experiences in the subcontinent has not found a place in this anthology perhaps because the exponents of the short story either are not particularly concerned with them, except as part of the social context, or because they prefer to deal with them in another literary form, more congenial to the theme of religion than the short story. Tagore, for example, mystically inclined as he was, expressed those thoughts in his poetry and songs while his short stories were urbane, sophisticated and witty. It is perhaps one of the perversities which make it so difficult to categorise authors that the one story in the anthology which can be called a study of a religious man is by Thakazhi Pillai, renowned for his exposés of the plight of 'untouchable' landless labourers and other exploited classes in his native Kerala!

This is a small selection and so the omissions are considerable. To have only fifteen stories for a multilingual subcontinent with fifteen major languages must, of necessity, mean the exclusion of many great names such as Manik Bandyopadhyay and Krishan Chander, Vaikom Basheer and Kartar Singh Duggal, Ismat Chugtai, Padmaraju, Mohan Rakesh, Qurrutulain Hyder and Meherunnissa Parvez. Again, to have left out totally anything from nine of the major regional languages only reveals the inadequacy of this or any other anthology which tries to sample the literature of a part of the globe encompassing some 900 million people. If the omissions provoke people to demand more anthologies, so much the better.

That the stories have to be read in translation is a necessity similar to the presentation of European literature. While a small minority of readers may read French or Russian literature in the original, the great majority of those who enjoy Proust or Tolstoy must go to translations. One hopes that a programme of translating the best writing from the subcontinent will become an established precedent to make available some very good pieces of creative work that remain inaccessible because they have not been translated or have been translated very badly. The Unesco series of Asian fiction, published in the late sixties and early seventies, should stimulate future ventures. Of course, should those whose appetite has been whetted through translated versions want to get the full flavour in the original, perhaps educational institutions will be prepared to make South Asian languages as much a part of the curriculum as the European languages are now.

To all who have helped in the compilation of these stories, the editor's grateful thanks. In particular to Mr Stephen Hoare of Harraps who first suggested the idea and gave help throughout; to Mr Ralph Russell, reader in Urdu, SOAS, University of London who so very kindly translated the story by Qasmi and made other helpful suggestions; to Mr Samik Bannerjee, Oxford University Press; to Mr Ashok Chatterji of the National Institute of Design; above all to Dr Krishna Kripalani, translator and biographer of Tagore and the first secretary of the Sahitya Akademi of India, which has brought regional literature to a wider public, for his incalculable help.

Where Indian words occur in the text they have been italicised the first time they appear. An explanation of each word may be found in the glossary on p.145. Other words and phrases thought to present difficulty have been marked by an asterisk and are explained in the notes on p.141.

JAMMU and KASHMIR
Kashmiri + Dogri

HIMACHAL
PRADESH

Lahore •

PUNJAB
Punjabi + Urdu

PAKISTAN
*Urdu + Punjabi,
Sindhi and Pushtu*

HARYANA
Punjabi + Hindi

Delhi

RAJASTHAN
Hindi + Rajasthani

Agra

UTTAR PRADESH
Hindi + Urdu

SIKKIM

ARUNACHAL
PRADESH

ASSAM
Assamese

NAGALAND

Karachi •

Varanasi •

MEGHALAYA

MANIPUR
Manipuri

Ahmedabad •

BIHAR
*Hindi + Maithili
and Tribal
Language*

BANGLADESH
Bengali

Dacca •

TRIPURA

MIZORAM

GUJARAT
Gujarati

MADHYA PRADESH
Hindi + Tribal Language

WEST
BENGAL
Bengali

Calcutta •

MAHARASHTRA
Marathi

ORISSA
Oriya

Bombay •

I N D I A

• Hyderabad

ANDHRA PRADESH
Telegu

KARNATAKA
Kannada

Bangalore •

• Madras

TAMIL NADU
Tamil

KERALA
Malayalam

• Madurai

SRI LANKA

Columbo •

General Reading List

Languages and Literature of India, Suniti Kumar Chatterji (Calcutta), Prakash Bhavan, 1963.

The Novel in India: its Birth and Development, Ed. T. W. Clark (London), George Allen and Unwin, 1970.

The Literatures of India, Ed. Edward Dimock (Chicago), University of Chicago Press, 1974. A historical perspective by several authors beginning with classical epic and drama, including poetry and fiction. The last chapter on the modern Hindi short story by Gordon Roadarmel is of special importance.

Critical Survey of Hindi Literature, R. A. Dwivedi (Delhi), Motital Banarsidas, 2nd ed. 1966.

Gujarat and its Literature, K. M. Munshi (Bombay), Bharatiya Vidya Bhavan, 1956.

History of Urdu Literature, Muhammad Sadiq (London), Oxford University Press, 1964.

Contemporary Literature: a Symposium (New Delhi), Sahitya Akademi, 1st series, 1957. Survey of the literature of 15 languages up to independence.

Indian Literature Since Independence: a Symposium (New Delhi), Sahitya Akademi, 1973. The contemporary scene as reflected in the literature of 20 languages.

Contemporary Writing in East Pakistan, Ed. Murshid Sarwar (Dacca), 1961.

History of Literature series, Sahitya Akademi: Titles include:

History of Bengali Literature, Sukmar Sen;

History of Gujerati Literature, Mansukhlal Jhaveri;

History of Kannada Literature, R. S. Mugali;

History of Malayalam Literature, P. K. Parmeswaran Nair;

Indian Literature, Sahitya Akademi. A bi-monthly journal containing literature and reviews.

Appeasement

Rabindranath Tagore (1861–1941)

Translated from the Bengali by Mary Lago, Tarun Gupta and Amiya
Chakravarty. From *The Housewarming and other Selected Writings of Tagore,*
edited by Amiya Chakravarty (Westport, Conn.) Greenwood Publishers,
1977

In his lifetime, Tagore was the greatest literary figure in the subcontinent.
Though almost forty years have elapsed since his death in 1941, his genius
is continually evoked and not only in his native Bengal. Of aristocratic
descent, Rabindranath came from a highly talented family. His creative
genius embraced poetry, prose, music and painting. A desire to reform
education led to his founding at Santiniketan, West Bengal, a school (now
the university of Viswa Bharati) where pupils would taste freedom and
where art and music were central. He was awarded the Nobel Prize for
literature in 1913 mainly for his poems, translated in a volume entitled
Gitanjali. Knighted by the British Government in 1915, he returned the
knighthood during the struggle for national freedom when a particularly
brutal act of repression, the Jalianwala Bagh massacre, incensed Indian
public opinion.

His poetry, lyrical and mystical, is quite removed from his worldly
stories and novels. He wrote almost a hundred stories—the last one a few
months before his death—and created a galaxy of interesting characters
drawn mainly from the upper class. There are many volumes of his stories
in translation as well as the standard biography by Krishna Kripalani.
Appeasement, written in 1895, is certainly not one of his most popular
works, at least for selection in anthologies. It concerns the age-old double
standard of morality where the husband can enjoy himself with wine,
women and song while the wife must face the lonely seclusion of the home.

Gopinath Sil's wife, Giribala, lived on the top floor of Ramanath
Sil's big three-storeyed house. A few jasmine plants and a rosebush
grew in a pot by the bedroom door. The terrace was surrounded by
a high wall; a few bricks had been removed here and there to

provide a view. In the bedroom hung many framed engravings of European actresses in different costumes but they were no lovelier than the reflection of the sixteen-year-old lady of the house that appeared in the big mirror by the door.

Giribala's beauty was like an unexpected burst of light, a sudden surprise, an awakening. It made an instant impression and was quite overwhelming. The beholder would think that he was not prepared for this; she was so different.

Giribala was conscious of her own loveliness. Her youth and beauty overflowed her body as wine foams and overflows the glass. She was inordinately concerned with her clothes and carriage, her gestures, the angle of her neck, the quick rhythm of her step. It was all her own: the music of her ankle bells, the jingling of her bracelets, her rippling laughter, her vivacious manner of speaking, her flashing eyes.

Giribala was intoxicated by her own beauty. Dressed in a pastel-shaded *sari,* she walked on the terrace. Her body felt an urge to dance to the rhythm of an indistinct, unknown song. She seemed to take pleasure in every movement as she stretched, whirled and turned. As she stirred up the waves of her own beauty, she felt the ebb and flow of extraordinary excitement in her blood. She would suddenly tear off some rose petals and with her right arm toss them skyward to be carried off by the wind. Her bracelets jingled, the end of her sari fluttered loose, the movement of her lovely arm was like that of a caged bird set free and flying away into the boundless cloud kingdom of the sky. All at once, she would pick up a lump of earth from the pot and throw it away for no apparent reason. Standing on tiptoe, she could peep through the wall for a quick glimpse of the great outside world. The end of her sari would twirl as she moved and the bunch of keys tied to it would clink and jingle. Perhaps she would stand in front of the mirror and let her hair down at midday. Raising her arms and holding a black ribbon between her teeth, she would coil her hair firmly into a braid at the back of her head. When she had nothing more to do, she would stretch lazily on the soft bed like a shaft of moonlight that had slipped through the leaves of the trees.

She had no children and no housework in this wealthy home.

She spent her days alone till she could stand it no longer. She had a husband but he was beyond her control. He did not notice that Giribala had left childhood behind and blossomed into a beauty. He had paid more attention to her as a little girl. In those days he would give his dozing tutor the slip and run away from school for an afternoon alone with his girl-wife. He wrote her letters on fancy stationery, even though they lived in the same house. He proudly showed those letters to his friends at school.

About this time, Gopinath's father died and Gopinath became the head of the house. The worm quickly penetrates the unseasoned wood. Young Gopinath soon found himself the prey of all sorts of odd creatures. His outside distractions increased and his visits to the inner rooms* became less frequent. There is excitement in leadership. Men are stimulated by the company of other men. Like Napoleon who felt compelled to extend his power over countless men and the panorama of history, this minor head of a minor salon had a compulsion to create a miniature empire out of his own little circle. It was exciting to collect a crowd of loafers as his regular cronies, wield influence over them and cheer them on. He was prepared to shoulder all the failures, debts and scandals in his mighty task.

Gopinath found the leadership of his clique increasingly stimulating. He grew more jovial every day, more proud of himself. His cronies began to say, 'Gopinath's more fun than anyone else!' His pride and excitement blinded him to all other considerations of pain, pleasure or duty. The misguided fellow was spun around and swallowed up as by a whirlpool.

Giribala, for her part, was enthroned in her empty bedroom. Her conquering beauty ruled over an untenanted kingdom. She was well aware that the gods had awarded her the sceptre and one glance from her would subjugate the wild world that she saw through the chink in the wall, but so far she had not been able to capture a soul in that world.

Giribala had a maidservant named Sudho. She sang, danced, recited jingles, praised her mistress's beauty and fretted over a heedless husband's neglect of such beauty. Giribala could not have managed without Sudho; she would listen to the lengthy eulogies of her own beautiful face, the shape of her figure and her fair complexion. Now and then she would protest and scold Sudho with a great show of disgust, calling her a liar and flatterer. Sudho would proclaim on her honour that no one was more innocent than she and Giribala was very easily convinced.

Sudho sang 'I've enslaved myself at your feet.' Giribala, listening to the praises of her own beautiful lac-tinted feet, conjured up in her imagination the picture of a slave prostrate before them but, alas, although two exquisite feet could make the empty terrace resound triumphantly with the music of their anklets, no one came of his own free will to write her a bond of indenture.

Gopinath had signed himself over to a girl named Labanya. She was an actress with a marvellous aptitude for fainting on the stage. When she panted and whimpered in her nasal, stagey voice and lisped, 'Lord of my heart!' the audience, dressed in waist coats, fine *dhotis* and long socks, would stand up and shout in English, 'Excellent! Excellent!'

Giribala's husband had already given her many glowing descriptions of the wonderful Labanya. But even though Giribala was unaware of her husband's infatuation, she was jealous that some other woman possessed the art which she did not of attracting her husband. Giribala often expressed a desire, which arose from an envious curiosity, to be taken to the theatre but she could never get Gopinath to agree. Finally, one day she gave Sudho the price of a ticket and sent her to see the play. Sudho came back frowning, fervently taking God's name and declaring that actresses should be disposed of with the broom and that the same treatment should be meted out to all those men who drooled over their disgusting figures and artificial ways. Giribala was greatly reassured.

But when Gopinath became footloose, her doubts revived. If she appeared sceptical about Sudho's words, Sudho would say that Labanya's figure was ungainly and dried up like a dressed-up piece of firewood. Giribala could not find out the secret of the actress's magnetic power and was hurt by the blow to her pride.

At last, she took Sudho with her and sneaked off to the theatre. The special thrill of things forbidden made her heart flutter. The lights, the crowded hall, the sound of music, the brightly-coloured scenery, all were magnified in splendour in her eyes. She was transported from those walled-in, joyless rooms of hers to this happy, well-dressed, festive crowd. The whole thing was like a dream.

The play that evening was *Appeasement*. When the bell rang, the music stopped and the restless audience quietened down. The footlights brightened, the curtain rose and a troupe of dancers, beautifully attired as women of Braj,* began to sway in time to the song. The theatre shook with the noise of prolonged applause and cheers. Giribala's blood began to race and surge through her young body. The rhythm, lights and dazzle, the chorus of praises made her momentarily forget society, the world, everything. She felt that she had found a haven that promised glorious deliverance from bondage.

Now and then Sudho would whisper, 'Madam, let's go back now. If master hears of this nothing'll save us.' Giribala paid no heed. She was not a bit afraid now. The play was very long. Radha was terribly piqued by Krishna* who could make no headway in this sea of resentment. How he pleaded, implored and wept! It was useless. Giribala was bursting with an inner pride. At the sight of Krishna's humiliation, she imagined herself as Radha with un-limited power. No one had ever humoured her as Krishna humoured Radha. She was an ignored, despised and deserted wife. Still, in that one extaordinary moment of delusion, she too had the power to be cruel and to make someone weep. She had heard that beauty had power and strength and now she saw it all very clearly by the light of the lamps, in the tunes of the songs. Her whole being was intoxicated.

At last the curtain fell, the gaslights were turned down, and the audience thinned out. Giribala sat there as if bewitched. She forgot that she would have to go home. Nothing existed except Krishna's downfall at the hands of Radha. When she returned to her bedroom it was very late. A lamp flickered in one corner but no one stirred. Only the mosquito net over her empty bed swished in the breeze. Her familiar world seemed very ugly, bleak and mean-ingless. Where was that world of beauty and lights and music where her own beauty could be diffused to fill the centre of the universe, where she would not be just a neglected, insignificant wife?

Now she began to go to the theatre every week. With time her first enchantment faded. Now she saw through the make-up and the artificiality but she was still fascinated by it all. When the curtain rose, her heart pounded like a soldier's at the sound of martial music. Where could a world-conquering beauty queen find a better throne than the lofty stage, bordered with gold letters, filled with the magic of poetry and music, the focus of enthralled spectators, and mysterious with the secrets of the greenroom?

The first time that she saw her husband in the audience, raving over the performance of some actress, she was bitter. She wanted that day to come when he would have to fall at her feet like a singed moth, drawn by her beauty, and she could walk out on him, showing her contempt in every part of her body. Then her wasted youth and beauty would be put to some good use. But that hoped-for day did not come. It became difficult even to catch a glimpse of Gopinath. He was whirled off like a dust-eddy into the storm of his own infatuation and no one knew of his whereabouts.

One night in mid-April Giribala, in a yellow sari, whose bordered end floated in the south wind, sat on the terrace. Although her husband did not come home these days, she had decked herself out in her latest jewellery. Her fingers and toes, covered with diamonds and pearls, dazzled as she moved. With a necklace of rubies and pearls and a sapphire ring on her little finger, she was a surge of glitter. Sudho sat on the floor and occasionally stroked Giribala's soft, rounded feet, *henna*-tinted. She sighed deeply and said, 'Oh madam, if I were a man I'd let myself be trampled to death by these feet.'

Giribala laughed haughtily. 'It seems as if no one's going to let himself be trampled so what else can be done with feet? Anyway, don't just sit there. Sing that song.'

On the lonely rooftop, flooded with moonlight, Sudho sang,

'I am enslaved by your beautiful feet,

The people of Vrindavan are my witnesses.'

It was ten o'clock. Everyone in the house had had dinner and gone to bed. Gopinath suddenly arrived, his scarf flying and reeking of perfume. Sudho hurriedly pulled up her veil and fled. Giribala thought that her day had come. She did not look up but remained seated like Radha, profoundly aloof. But the scene did not proceed. The peacock's tail did not collapse at her feet and nobody sang, 'Why does the full moon hide its face?'

In a dry voice Gopinath said, 'Give me your keys.'

In the spring moonlight, after such a long separation, what kind of opening line was this? Did those who wrote poetry and drama produce nothing but lies? A stage lover would have fallen at her feet singing his lament but this fellow had come in the middle of the night to his own incomparable wife only to ask for her keys!

The south wind blew, sighing for the wasted romance of the situation; the fragrance from the jasmine swept across the roof. Giribala's humiliation showed in her wide-open eyes and the scented edge of her yellow sari fluttered frantically. She abandoned all pride. Taking his hands she said, 'I'll give you the keys when you come inside.' She was determined to make him beg and she would bring forth her invincible weapons and triumph.

'I can't stay long,' said Gopinath. 'Give me the keys.'

'I'll give them to you and all that goes with them but you can't go out tonight.'

'That's impossible. I've got urgent business.'

'Then I won't give them to you,' she said.

'Oh, won't you just! I'll see if you don't.' He saw there were no keys tied to the end of her sari so he went into the room, opened the dressing-table drawer but the keys were not there. He smashed open her toilet case. It contained a jar of mascara, a box of vermilion, hair ribbons and an assortment of similar items—but no keys. Then he tore the mattress, forced open the wardrobe and ransacked it. She sat as stiff as a stone image. The frustrated Gopinath, growling angrily, went up to her. 'I told you to give me the keys. You'll be sorry if you don't.' She said not a word. Then he pushed her, pulled off her bracelets, necklace and ring, gave her a kick and made his exit.

No one in the house awoke. No one in the vicinity knew anything about it. The moonlit night was as silent as ever. Peace was undisturbed. Giribala's heart was torn in complete silence.

Somehow she endured the night. She was not going to report such a defeat to Sudho. She contemplated suicide, of destroying her matchless beauty with her own hands. But she remembered that nobody would benefit by such an act nor would anybody feel the least distress. There was neither pleasure in life nor consolation in death. 'I'll go to my father's,' she thought. He lived a long way from Calcutta. She paid no attention to her mother-in-law's objections and refused to take anyone with her. Gopinath was away on a boating trip with his friends.

2.

Gopinath's love for the theatre made him go there every day. Labanya was appearing as Manorama in a play by that name and Gopinath and his cronies were sitting in the best orchestra seats. 'Bravo!' they shouted and tossed bouquets on the stage. The audience began to get very annoyed by these daily interruptions but the managers did not have the courage to stop them. One day, Gopinath who was a little drunk, went into the greenroom and caused a big commotion. He felt insulted by some imaginary slight and slapped an actress viciously. Her shrieks and Gopinath's abusive words startled the entire theatre.

That day, the managers could stand it no longer and got the police to throw Gopinath out. He vowed revenge. For a month before the Puja holidays,* the theatre management had been publicising, with considerable fanfare, the opening of their new play, *Manorama*. At this point Gopinath took off on a boating trip with their leading lady, Labanya. She disappeared—nobody knew where—and their search produced no results. They waited for her for a few days and then began to train a new actress for the title role. This caused a slight delay in their production schedule but no real damage had been done. The regular theatregoers were not deterred. They came back by the hundreds and there was no end to the praise in the newspapers.

Gopinath heard the chorus of praise in the far reaches of the country and could stay away no longer. Full of spite and curiosity he came to see the play. In the first act, Manorama appeared as a drudge in her father-in-law's home. Humble and destitute, she did not speak a single line and her face could not be seen very clearly. In the last act she was sent back to her father's house by her greedy husband, now about to re-marry the only daughter of a millionaire. After the wedding, when the husband looked beneath his wife's veil in the bridal chamber, he found that the bride was Manorama. No longer a drudge, she was dressed like a princess. Her peerless beauty, heightened by the splendour of her clothes and jewels, shone radiantly. Manorama had been kidnapped from her wealthy home as a child and raised in a poor family. When her father found her and brought her home, he had her re-married with all the pomp of her real status to her own husband.

Then began the whole business of reconciliation between Manorama and her husband while in the audience a frightful row had broken out. As long as Manorama's face had been concealed under the shabby clothes of a domestic servant, Gopinath had watched quietly. But when she stood as a bride, glittering in her jewels and red wedding sari, the veil thrown off and her beauty revealed; when she turned with an indescribable pride and dignity to face the audience and Gopinath, and withered him with a look like a lightning bolt, when the entire audience joined in prolonged applause that shook the theatre—then Gopinath suddenly leapt to his feet shouting, 'Giribala! Giribala!' He tried to jump on to the stage but the musicians held him back.

The members of the audience were furious at this abrupt interruption of their enjoyment and began to shout in English and Bengali, 'Get him away! Throw him out!' Like a madman Gopinath kept shouting hoarsely, 'I'll murder her, I'll murder her.' The police came, arrested Gopinath and took him out. The entire city of Calcutta went to feast its eyes on Giribala's acting. Gopinath was the only one who was refused admission.

Reading List

Rabindranath Tagore: a Biography, Krishna Kripalani (London), Oxford University Press, 1962

My Boyhood Days, Rabindranath Tagore, translated by Marjorie Sykes (Calcutta), Viswa Bharati, 1945

There are many anthologies of translations of Tagore's short stories as well as some of his poetry and excerpts from novels:

The Boundless Sky (Calcutta), Viswa Bharati, 1964;

The Housewarming and other Selected Writings, translated and edited by Amiya Chakravarty *et al* (New York), New American Library, 1965

Among the novels are *Binodini,* translated by Krishna Kripalani (New Delhi), Sahitya Akademi, 1959 and *The Broken Nest,* translated by Mary Lago and Supriya Bari, Macmillan, India, 1971. The latter was made into a moving film by Satyajit Ray under the title of *Charulata.*

January Night

Premchand (1880–1936)

Translated from the Hindi by David Rubin. From *The World of Premchand*
(London), Allen and Unwin, Unesco Asian Fiction Series, 1969

Premchand was the *nom de plume* of Dhanpat Rai Srivastava, the greatest
figure in Hindi fiction and a master of the short story. He wrote nearly 300
stories—first in Urdu and then in Hindi. Through them, Premchand
established the modern form of the Indian short story. He wrote about the
villages in the eastern districts of what was then known as United
Provinces and is now called Uttar Pradesh. His intention was to use
literature to arouse people's enthusiasm for change, and his own commit-
ment to social ideals became more radical over the years. His greatest novel
Godaan is an epic of the struggle of the Indian peasant against economic and
social exploitation, while many of his village stories, including *January
Night,* deal with similar themes though not in a didactic vein. His skill in
creating memorable characters and, above all, his language—simple yet
highly metaphorical, distilling the allusions and proverbs of the people—
elevated his social realism to majestic heights.

Halku, the poor peasant in this story which was first published in 1930,
tries hard to hold on to what little land he has but fails and joins the ranks of
the agricultural labourers.

Halku came in and said to his wife, 'The landlord's come. Get the
rupees you set aside. I'll give him the money and somehow or other
we'll get along without it.'

Munni had been sweeping. She turned around and said, 'But
there are only three rupees. If you give them to him, where's the
blanket going to come from? How are you going to get through
these January nights in the fields? Tell him we'll pay him after the
harvest, not right now.'

For a moment, Halku stood hesitating. January was on top of
them. Without a blanket, he could not possibly sleep in the fields at

night. But the landlord would not be put off; he'd threaten and insult him. So what did it matter if they died in the cold weather as long as they could just take care of this calamity right now? As he thought this, he moved his heavy body that gave the lie to his name★ and came close to his wife. Trying to coax her he said, 'Come on, give it to me. We'll manage. I'll figure out some other plan to get the blanket.'

Munni drew away from him. Her eyes angry, she said, 'You've already tried "Some other plan". You just tell me what other plan can be found. Is somebody going to give you a blanket? God knows how many debts are always left over that we can't pay off. What I say is, give up this tenant farming. The work's killing you. Whatever you harvest goes to pay up the arrears, so why not finish with it? Were we born just to keep paying off debts? Earn some money for your own belly, give up that kind of farming. I won't give you the money, I won't!'

Sadly Halku said, 'Then I'll have to put up with his abuse.'

Losing her temper, Munni said, 'Why should he abuse you—is this his kingdom?'

But as she said it, her brows relaxed from the frown. The bitter truth in Halku's words came charging at her like a wild beast.

She went to the niche in the wall, took out the rupees and handed them over to Halku. Then she said, 'Give up farming this time. If you work as a hired labourer you'll get enough food to eat from it. No one will be yelling insults at you. Fine work, farming someone else's land! Whatever you earn you throw back into it and get insulted into the bargain.'

Halku took the money and went outside looking as though he were tearing his heart out and giving it away. He'd saved the rupees from his work, *pice* by pice, for his blanket. Today he was going to throw it away. With every step, his head sank lower under the burden of his poverty.

2.

A dark January night. In the sky, even the stars seemed to be shivering. At the edge of his field, underneath a shelter of cane leaves, Halku lay on a bamboo cot wrapped up in his old sacking, shivering. Underneath the cot his friend, Jabra the dog, was whimpering with his muzzle pressed into his belly. Neither one of them was able to sleep. Halku curled up, drawing his knees close against his chin, and said, 'Cold, Jabra? Didn't I tell you in the house you could lie in the paddy straw? So why did you come out here? Now you'll have to bear the cold, there's nothing I can do. You thought I was coming out here to eat *puris* and sweets and came running ahead of me. Now you can moan all you want.'

Jabra wagged his tail without getting up, protracted his whimpering into a long yawn and was silent. Perhaps in his canine wisdom he guessed that his whimpering was keeping his master awake.

Halku reached out his hand and patted Jabra's cold back. 'From tomorrow on, stop coming with me or the cold'll get you. This bitch of a west wind comes from nobody-knows-where, bringing the icy cold with it. Let me get up and fill my pipe. I've smoked eight pipefuls already but we'll get through the night somehow. This is the reward you get for farming. Some lucky fellows are lying in houses where if the cold comes the heat just drives it away. A good thick quilt, warm covers, blankets! Just let the winter cold try to get them! Fortune's arranged everything very well. While we do the hard work somebody else gets the joy of it.'

He got up, took some embers from the pit and filled his pipe. Jabra got up too.

Smoking, Halku said, 'If you smoke, the cold's just as bad but at least you feel better.'

Jabra looked at him with eyes overflowing with love.

'You've got to put up with just one more cold night. Tomorrow I'll spread some straw. When you bed down in that you won't feel the cold.'

Jabra put his paws on Halku's knees and brought his muzzle close. Halku felt his warm breath. After he finished smoking, Halku lay down and made up his mind that, however bad things were, he would sleep now. But in only one minute his heart began to pound. He turned from side to side. Like some kind of witch, the cold weather continued to torment him. When he could bear it no longer, he gently picked Jabra up and, patting his head, got him to fall asleep in his lap. The dog's body gave off some kind of stench but Halku, hugging him tight, experienced a happiness he had not felt for months. Jabra probably thought he was in heaven, and in Halku's innocent heart there was no resentment of his smell. He embraced him with the very same affection he would have felt for a brother or a friend. He was not crippled by the poverty which had reduced him to these straits at present. Rather, it was as though this singular friendship had opened all the doors to his heart and brilliantly illuminated every atom of it.

Suddenly, Jabra picked up the noise of some animal. This special intimacy had produced a new alertness in him that disdained the onslaught of the wind. Springing up, he ran out of the shelter and began to bark. Halku whistled and called him several times. But Jabra would not come back to him. He went on barking while he ran around through the furrows of the field. He would come back for a moment, then dash off again at once. The sense of duty had taken possession of him as though it were desire.

Another hour passed. The night fanned up the cold with the wind. Halku sat up and, bringing both knees tight against his chest, hid his face between them but the cold was just as biting. It seemed as though all his blood had frozen, that ice rather than blood filled his veins. He leaned back to look at the skies. How much of the night was still left! The Dipper had not yet climbed half the sky. By the time it was overhead it would probably be morning. Night would last another three hours or so.

Only a stone's throw from Halku's field there was a mango grove. The leaves had begun to fall and they were heaped up in the grove. Halku thought, 'If I go and get a pile of leaves I can make a fire and keep warm. If anybody sees me gathering the leaves in the dead of night they'll think it's a ghost. Of course there's a chance some animal's hidden in my field waiting, but I can't put up with sitting here any longer.' He ripped up some stalks from a nearby field, made a broom out of them and picking up a lighted cowdung cake* went toward the grove. Jabra watched him coming and ran to him, wagging his tail.

Halku said, 'I couldn't stand it any more, Jabra. Come along, let's go into the orchard and gather leaves to warm up with. When we're toasted, we'll come back and sleep. The night's still far from over.'

Jabra barked his agreement and trotted on towards the orchard. Under the trees it was pitch dark and in the darkness the bitter wind blew, buffeting the leaves, and drops of dew dripped from the branches. Suddenly, a gust carried the scent of henna blossom to him. 'Where's that sweet smell coming from, Jabra? Or can't your nose make out anything as fragrant as this?'

Jabra had found a bone lying somewhere and he was chewing on it. Halku set his fire down on the ground and began to gather the leaves. In a little while, he had a great heap. His hands were frozen, his bare feet numb. But he'd piled up a regular mountain of leaves and by making a fire out of them he would burn away the cold. In a little while, the fire was burning merrily. The flames leapt upward licking at the overhanging branches. In the flickering light, the immense trees of the grove looked as though they were carrying the vast darkness on their heads. In the blissful sea of darkness, the firelight seemed to pitch and toss like a boat.

Halku sat before the fire and let it warm him. After a while, he took off his shawl and tucked it behind him, then he spread out both feet as though challenging the cold to do its worst. Victorious over the immense power of winter, he could not repress his pride in his triumph. He said to Jabra, 'Well, Jabra, you're not cold now, are you?'

Jabra barked as if to say, 'How could I feel cold now?'

'We should have thought of this plan before, then we'd never have become so chilled.' Jabra wagged his tail. 'Fine, now what say we jump over the fire? Let's see how we manage it. But if you get scorched I've got no medicine for you.'

Jabra looked fearfully at the fire.

'We musn't tell Munni tomorrow or there'll be a row.'

With that he jumped up and cleared the fire in one leap. He got his legs singed but he did not care. Jabra ran around the fire and came up to him. Halku said, 'Go on, no more of this. Jump over the fire!' He leaped again and came back to the other side.

The leaves were all burned up. Darkness covered the orchard

again. Under the ashes a few embers smouldered and when a gust of wind flew over them they stirred up briefly, then flickered out again.

Halku wrapped himself up in his shawl again and sat by the warm ashes, humming a tune. The fire had warmed him through but as the cold began to spread he felt drowsy. Jabra gave a loud bark and ran towards the field. Halku realised that this meant a pack of wild animals had probably broken into the field. They might be bluebuck. He distinctly heard the noise of their moving about. Then it seemed to him they must be grazing; he began to hear the sound of nibbling. He thought, 'No, with Jabra around no animal can get into the field; he'd rip it to shreds. I must've been mistaken. Now there's no sound at all. I must have been mistaken?'

He shouted, 'Jabra! Jabra!' Jabra went on barking and did not come to him.

Then again there was the sound of munching and crunching in the field. He could not have been mistaken this time. It really hurt to think about getting up from where he was. It was so comfortable there that it seemed intolerable to go to the field in this cold and chase after animals. He did not stir. He shouted at the top of his lungs, 'Hillo! Hillo! Hillo!'

Jabra started barking again. There were animals eating in his field just when the crop was ready. What a fine crop it was! And those cursed animals were destroying it. With a firm resolve he got up and took a few steps. But suddenly a gust of wind pierced him with a sting like a scorpion's so that he went back and sat again by the extinguished fire and stirred up the ashes to warm his chilled body.

Jabra was barking his lungs out, the bluebuck were devastating his field and Halku went on sitting peacefully near the warm ashes. His drowsiness held him motionless as though with ropes. Wrapped in his shawl, he fell asleep on the warmed ground near the ashes.

When he woke in the morning, the sun was high and Munni was saying, 'Do you think you're going to sleep all day? You came out here and had a fine time while the whole field was being flattened!'

Halku got up and said, 'Then you've just come from the field?'

'Yes, the whole field's ruined. And you could sleep like that!

Why did you bother to put up the shelter anyway?'

Halku sought an excuse. 'I nearly died and just managed to get through the night and you worry about your crop. I'd such a pain in my belly that I can't describe it.'

Then the two of them walked to the edge of their land. He looked: the whole field had been trampled and Jabra was stretched out underneath the shelter as though he were dead.

They continued to stare at the ruined field. Munni's face was shadowed with grief but Halku was content. She said, 'Now you'll have to hire yourself out to earn some money to pay off the rent and taxes.'

With a contented smile Halku said, 'But I won't have to sleep nights out here in the cold.'

Further Reading

The World of Premchand, translated by David Rubin (London), Allen and Unwin, 1969.

The Chess Players and Other Stories, translated by Gurdial Singh (New Delhi), Orient Paperbacks (*The Chess Players* was made into a film by Satyajit Ray in 1977.)

Premchand's major novel about the life of a village, *Godaan,* translated as *The Gift of a Cow* by Gordon Roadarmel is part of the Unesco Asian fiction series, Allen and Unwin, 1968.

There are two biographies available in English:

Munshi Premchand: a Literary Biography, Madan Gopal (Bombay), Asia Publishing House, 1974

Munshi Premchand of Lamhi Village, Robert O. Swan (Durham, N. Carolina), Duke University Press, 1969

A concise critique on Premchand is available in translation:

Premchand, Prakash Chandra Gupta from 'The Makers of Indian Literature' series, (New Delhi), Sahitya Akademi, 1977.

Tarini the Boatman

Tarashankar Bandyopadhyay (1898–1971)

Translated from the Bengali by Hiren Mukherji. From *Contemporary Indian Short Stories, Vol II* (New Delhi), Sahitya Akademi, 1977

Tarashankar Bandyopadhyay, novelist, short story writer and dramatist, is considered to be one of the great trio of novelists in Bengali literature after Tagore, the other two being Sarat Chandra Chattopadhyay and Bibhutibhushan Bandyopadhyaya, the author of *Pather Panchali*. Tarashankar's novels and stories are essentially about rural life in Birbhum, a district of West Bengal. His most outstanding novels, like *Five Villages* and *The Legend of the Sickle-bend,* deal with the various classes and castes who live in the village and show the changes that are overtaking them—the decline of the rural aristocracy, the decay of rural artisans and the loss of their holdings by peasants who have to seek work in nearby railway yards or factories. His treatment of the down-trodden semi-tribal field labourers and his use of their dialect have enriched modern Bengali literature and language. Many of his short stories, which were written before his major novels, are also about ordinary villagers but he sees the conflict of emotions and passions underneath their poverty and traditional conformity.

Tarini, the boatman, always walked with a stoop. Uncommonly tall, he had too often bumped his head against branches and the split bamboo ceilings of huts and had learnt his lesson. But on the river, rowing his palm-bark ferry boat with a very long pole, he would hold himself absolutely erect.

It was during the rainy season in the month of *Asharh*. Pilgrims were coming back after their holy dip in the Ganges on the occasion of the Ambubachi festival.* A tired crowd, mostly old women, hurried homewards across the Mayurakshi.

Tarini finished his smoke and shouted, 'I can't take any more of you, mothers. You're all so heavy with the load of your piety.'

'Just one more, please, good man,' pleaded an old woman. 'This

little boy . . .,' while another called out to a friend, 'Come along
Sabi, come quickly. Stop jabbering and laughing. We don't want
to see those witch's teeth any longer.'

Sabi or Savitri, joking and giggling with a crowd of girls from
nearby villages, called out, 'You go ahead, we'll go together on the
next trip.'

The boatman retorted, 'No, you're coming on this one. If you
lot stay together, my boat's sure to sink.'

'If it must sink, Tarini,' said the girl, 'better let it go down with
the old people. They've all bathed in the Ganges ten or twelve
times, and they don't mind dying because they'll go straight to
heaven. This has been my first pilgrimage, you see.'

'I see, mother,' said Tarini,' you're all full of Ganges water.' The
passengers began to laugh and the boatman jumped on to the ferry
while his mate, Kalachand, started collecting the fares.

Tarini pushed off. 'God be praised,' he shouted as he pushed his
pole against the river bank. The pilgrims took up the cry and the
woods on both shores resounded with it while the swift-flowing
river seemed to respond with a low mocking laugh.

'Blast you, Kala, can't you get a good grip on the rudder?'
growled Tarini. 'You don't eat rice, it seems. Can't you see the
current you fool?'

Tarini was right. The Mayurakshi is famous for its strong
current. For seven or eight months in the year the river is a desert,
its sands stretching from shore to shore for a mile and a half. But
when the rains come, she is terrible, like a demon. She races along,
four or five miles wide, her deep, grey water covering everything
within reach. Once in a while there is a flood, when the water, six
or seven metres deep, rushes into the villages and washes away
homes and granaries and all else in its way. This does not happen
very often, though. The last time was about twenty years ago.

The sun by now was oppressive and a passenger opened his
umbrella. 'Don't put your sail up,' advised Tarini, 'you'll fly away
in the wind.' The man shut his umbrella promptly.

Suddenly, there came a shriek from the river and everyone in the
boat looked around in consternation. 'Be careful, all of you,'
shouted Tarini. 'A boat's sinking near Olkura landing stage. Hi, old

mother, why're you trembling?' Then, turning to the man with the umbrella, he said, 'I say, Thakur, look after her. There's nothing to be afraid of; we're almost across. Kala, hold this pole and be quick.' The next minute, Tarini had jumped into the water and was swimming towards the boat. The old women began to wail. 'What'll happen to us with Tarini gone?'

'Shut up, you old hags,' stormed Kalachand. 'Don't call out to him or you'll be dead, you'll be dead.'

An object could be seen bobbing up and down in the grey water ahead. Tarini swam towards it quickly with easy strokes. When he drew close, he dived down and as he came up he was seen pulling something with one hand and swimming with the other. The crowd on the shore was watching him with fear and anxiety. They cried out, 'God be praised!' and from the other side came the cry, 'Is everything all right? Is everything all right?' Kalachand drew close to Tarini.

Tarini was lucky. The girl he had rescued belonged to a prosperous family of the locality. Her boat was in no danger but she had moved too close to the edge and because she had pulled her *sari* well over her face like a veil, she had not been able to see and toppled over. She had swallowed some water but not too much and was soon nursed back to consciousness. Barely sixteen and pretty, she wore a lot of jewellery including nose-ring, bangles and a necklace. She was still gasping for breath when her husband and father-in-law arrived on the scene. Tarini bowed to both of them and the girl quickly drew her sari over her face. 'Don't be so bashful, mother,' Tarini said. 'Take a few deep breaths, It's your shyness that brought you all this trouble.'

'Tell me, Tarini,' said Ghosh Mahashay, the father-in-law, 'what would you like as a reward?'

Tarini scratched his head for a while and then muttered, 'Give me the price of a pot of brew—eight annas.'

'Don't be a fool,' Sabi shouted from the crowd. 'Can't you ask for something more worthwhile?'

Tarini looked as if he had only just taken in the situation and smiled in embarrassment. 'Let me have a big nose-ring, then sir.'

Sabi called out again. 'That's right, Tarini. How the wife will shake her jewelled nose when she talks!' The good-humoured crowd laughed.

The girl who had been rescued now put her hand out and there was a golden nose-ring, gleaming in the morning sun.

'Come over to our place during Dasahara*, Tarini,' said the father-in-law, 'and you'll get a *dhoti* and *chaddar*. And here's five *rupees.*'

Tarini bent low gratefully and mumbled, 'Sir, if you could give me a sari for the wife instead of a dhoti for me . . .'

'That's quite all right. You'll have a sari,' and the father-in-law laughed.

'Tarini, you must let us see your wife,' said the irrepressible Sabi.

'She's nothing much to look at really—dark and ugly.'

When Tarini walked homewards that night, he was dead drunk. Feeling his way along the road, he was grumbling, 'Who's dug these holes, Kala? Holes, holes, everywhere.' Kalachand, equally drunk, could only mumble agreement.

'Let's swim home,' Tarini went on 'Don't you see, these holes'll soon fill up with water. Damn! There's no water in them at all. 'Tarini walked on, flinging his arms about as if he were swimming.

His hut was in an outlying part of the village. There was Sukhi, his wife, waiting for him, holding a lamp. Tarini was trying to sing something about nose-rings but Sukhi stopped him. 'That's enough. Come and eat. The rice has gone cold and stiff.'

'Rice! Rice! Forget that now. You must put on the nose-ring first. Now where did I put it? He searched with uncertain fingers around the waistband of his *dhoti*.

'One of these days you'll go to save somebody and that'll be the end of you,' said Sukhi who had already heard of his feat that morning. 'I'll hang myself should that happen.'

'What have I done?' Tarini looked puzzled.

'Such a terrible flood . . . and you . . .'

His laughter started the deep dark of the rainy evening. 'Does one ever fear one's mother? The Mayurakshi is a mother to me, isn't she? Whatever food I get is because of her.'

Sukhi had not waited to listen but was busy getting his food.

'Why don't you listen?' Tarini shouted as he went towards the kitchen and caught her from behind. 'You've got to come with me right now and take a look at the river.'

'Don't be foolish and stop bothering me,'she said. But he insisted. 'You must come, yes, a hundred times yes. We'll go to the river and I'll jump in with you on my back and we'll come ashore at Panchthupi Ghat.'

'All right, all right,' Sukhi tried to humour him, 'But you must have your rice first.'

Tarini was going to flare up again but he bumped his head against the door and sobered up. Eating his rice he began, 'Didn't I rescue a couple of cows that time and that devil, Madan Gop, cheated me of fifteen rupees—fifteen rupees! A hell of a lot of money that was, five short of a score. Who gave you those bangles? Tell me which of your uncles was it? If that scoundrel Madan drowns in the river I'll make him swallow something before I pull him out, I will by God!'

Sukhi, meanwhile, was loosening his waistband and taking out the nose-ring and three rupees. 'What have you done with the other two rupees?' she demanded.

'Oh, I gave them to Kala.' His voice sounded guilty. 'The fellow was there, you know, and I told him to take the money.'

Sukhi knew where he had been but said nothing. She was not used to bandying words. Tarini began again,' That time—do you remember? You were ill and I wasn't plying the boat, the post was held up and the police officer couldn't go across and they had to summon me. I got you those two ear-rings out of my tips that time didn't I? The river's been good to me really.'

'Wait,' she said, 'let me put on the nose-ring.'

He was pleased and stopped his chatter. As his wife put it on with the aid of a little mirror, he stared at her, forgetting his food. When she had finished, he raised the lantern—even before washing his hands—and said, 'Let me have a good look at you Sukhi.'

Her face was transfigured with simple happiness. Tarini had lied to Savitri. Sukhi was pretty, slender and not very dark either. He was proud of her and happy.

Tarini was right. It was indeed the Mayurakshi that gave him his living. Every year, on Dasahara day, he would worship the river.

This year, too, he went to pay his homage. He had put on a new dhoti and Sukhi was wearing a new sari, both gifts from the grateful Ghosh family. The rains had not yet started; the sandy bed of the river was glistening in the brilliant summer sun. 'Worship her well, brother,' said Keshto Das of Bhogpur village. 'Let's have some good rain and floods too—farmers must live musn't they?'

The silt, deposited by the river when it overflowed both banks, produced golden crops.

'You're quite right,' smiled Tarini. 'Do you know what these people say? That I worship the river and beg for floods. They forget, the fools, that the river's our mother and brings wealth to our land.' His eyes turned to the goat about to be sacrificed.

'Don't let the goat run away, Kala.'

When the ceremony was over, Tarini began to drink heavily with his mate. 'This time,' said Kalachand, 'If anyone gets drowned I'll be the one to go and save him and get the reward.'

Tarini laughed loudly. 'What an idea! Kala to the rescue! Ha, ha!' Tarini was ready to have a go at him but Sukhi intervened and offered a compromise. 'When the floods come and should anyone start to drown on this side of the Pakur tree over there . . .' and she turned to her husband, 'you can save him. But if beyond that line,' and she turned to Kala, 'you can.' In a spasm of drunken gratitude Kalachand burst into tears and knelt at her feet. 'You're good, sister. There's no one like you.'

The next morning, the two set about repairing the boat. They worked till the evening and made it look like new. But the fierce sun soon made cracks in the bark. There were no floods throughout the month of *Asharh*, not even any heavy downpours to do more than wet the sand on the river bed. Disaster was in the air; one could hear, as it were, a low plaintive cry of thirst from the land. Tarini hardly earned enough to live on. He would get a few coppers when some minor official made him carry a bicycle across the sands but that hardly paid for his drinks. Government officials began to come often to the villages to enquire about the distress but they left nothing behind save shrivelled cigarette ends.

The rains did not come till the month of *Sravan*. Tarini breathed happily again and jumped into the river and swam with boyish exhilaration. After three days, however, the water was only knee-deep. Tarini and Kalachand were waiting with their boat tied to a tree in the hope that some gentleman might want to go across and they might push the boat along for him. It was nearly evening and no one had come. 'It's funny, Kala, look at the western sky. It's just blue with not a cloud anywhere and not a sound in the sky.'

'Yes, yes,' Kalachand agreed.

Tarini, in a sudden fury, slapped Kalachand. 'Yes, yes!' he mimicked. 'How I love to hear you say that.'

Kalachand looked stupidly at Tarini. He was embarrassed but not angry. Tarini felt he could not stand this much longer. He looked away and sat motionless. Suddenly, he turned round abruptly. 'The wind's changed, Kala. It's from the west . . . let me see.' Slowly, he threw some sand into the air to find out the wind's direction. 'Hm, it's from the west. Come on Kala, let's go and have a drink. I've got two annas. Pinched them from Sukhi's sari.'

Kalachand was elated by this cordial invitation. He followed Tarini. 'Your wife's still got some money left, Dada. You'll get your rice all right when you go home But I . . . I'm done for.'

Sukhi's a good girl, a very good girl. I don't know what I'd do without her.'

Suddenly, Kala ran off to pick up a *tal* at the foot of a toddy palm tree where a small group of people were squatting. They were from Birchandpur going to Burdwan.

We hope there'll be work for us there,' they said.

'Has there been much rain in Burdwan?' Kala asked.

'No, but there's an irrigation canal.'

Disaster struck soon. Famine had lain concealed under the earth and as the ground cracked in the fierce heat it showed its gruesome face. Farmers who had any stock of grain shut their doors to all customers. Poor peasants starved and people flocked out of their villages. That morning, Tarini went to the river but could not find Kalachand. He went to his hut, shouted out his name but there was no reply. He went into the hut and found not a soul. It was the same at the next hut. The entire neighbourhood had gone—left the night before.

Hari Mondol told Tarini, 'I asked him not to go but he said he would find a rich village and beg.'

Tarini had a lump in his throat. 'Are there any rich people left in the villages? They've either left or are in a bad way. They'll starve but not tell anyone out of pride. A gentleman in Palashdanga put a rope round his neck the other day. He'd nothing to eat, poor man.'

The next day he saw the corpse of an old woman. Jackals had torn off her limbs but he could recognise her as a paralytic. Perhaps her family had left her and hurried out of the stricken village. Tarini went straight home and told his wife to tie her jewellery round her waist as they must leave to find work in the town. When they were on the road he noticed that Sukhi had no ornaments. Surprised, he asked her what had happened to them. She smiled dryly, 'How do you think I ran the house all this time?'

They trudged for three days and took shelter for the night in a village. Two ripe *tals* which had dropped from a tree provided them with dinner. He hung her *gamcha* on a branch and watched it closely for the direction of the wind. At dawn she found him sitting in the same position. When she reproached him for neglecting his health he ignored her outburst but cried out, 'Sukhi, look! The ants are going up the trees with their eggs in their mouths. That means it's going to rain for sure.'

'You've got some funny ideas in your head, ' Sukhi said.

'You don't understand, Sukhi. They know when the rains are coming and take shelter. Look! There's a breeze coming up right now from the west.'

'But the sky's all dry and bright. You do have queer ideas.'

He was gazing at the far horizon. 'It doesn't take long for clouds to come over. The crows have started picking up dried twigs to make their nests secure. Let's stay here, Sukhi, and see if it rains.'

The boatman's practised observation proved correct. Towards the evening the sky was overcast and the wind blew strong. He told Sukhi they would go back. 'Now?' she asked.

'Yes. You're not afraid of the dark are you dear? I'm here. Come along. Put that *mathali* on your head. Drizzle can be dangerous.'

'What about you? I suppose your body's made of stone.'

He laughed. 'The rain's my friend, you know. I bask in the sun and revel in the rain. Come along then. Give me that load.'

It rained hard for some time and then when the wind rose again it came down in torrents. When they reached home and Tarini went to see the river, he was full of joy as the water was nearly overflowing its banks. Next day he took Sukhi to see the river. The tumultuous beauty of the Mayurakshi was fascinating. You could hardly see the other bank. The water was a saffron colour and the white foam looked like sweeeping masses of flowers. 'You can hear her roar and it'll grow worse.' That evening there was worry on his face. What was that 'doog, doog' sound? Impending danger. The floods were coming and not the sort that was good for his trade.

He had to pass a bamboo bridge over a usually innocuous tributary of the Mayurakshi. Generally he could walk home blindfolded but this time he could not find the bridge. Where it should have been there was oily water. He could hear a disquieting roar, the swish of the wind. Insects crawled all over his body. Even they were coming out of their holes in a vain search for safety. He had to swim through the waist-deep water everywhere. Some of the villagers, holding on to any solid object for support were shouting for help and their cows and goats, sheep and dogs moaned. And above all the roar of the Mayurakshi and the cruel laughter of the wind as if plundering *dacoits* were howling down the piteous cries of their victims.

The water was waist deep in their courtyard. Sukhi stood, fear in her eyes, clutching a bamboo. He dragged her by the arm. 'What are you doing here? The house'll collapse any minute.'

'I was waiting for you. Where else could you've found me?'

'What can we do, Sukhi?' his voice trembled.

'Don't worry,' she said. 'Everybody's in the same plight.'

'What if the flood rises higher? Can you hear that roar?'

'It can't,' she said with a woman's nonchalance. 'What'll happen to the country, then? God can't destroy his own creation, can he?'

Tarini tried to find consolation in the mysteries of providence but could not. Suddenly there was a heavy splash. 'Help! My baby's gone. My baby!'

'I'll go,' Tarini cried, reckless as ever.

After a while, he called out to Sukhi and when he heard her voice went towards her. 'It looks bad, Sukhi. Hold on to my waist.' She caught hold of her husband's dhoti. 'Whose child was it? Could you save him?' she asked.

Yes. It was Bhupte Bhalla's boy.'

They were wading carefully through the water. It got more and more difficult. 'Get on to my back, Sukhi,' he said. 'But where are we? Where?'

They were moving fast in the current. It was pitch dark. The sharp whistling of the wind mingled with the uncanny roar of the flood. They were floating like bundles of straw, for how long they did not know. Their limbs were getting stiff and the cruel waves almost suffocated them. Sukhi's grip felt strange, thought Tarini. She was getting heavier too, terribly heavy.

'Sukhi,' he gasped.

'Yes,' was her dazed reply.

'Don't be afraid, my love.'

The next moment, he knew he was drowning, going round and round in a whirl. He could not be beaten though, not by the river he loved. But Sukhi . . . with all his strength he managed to reach the surface with her. There was the whirlpool and he fought to get away from it, but Sukhi was clasping him tight with her arms. 'Sukhi, Sukhi,' he implored. There was no reply.

They were going round and round again. They were drowning. Tarini felt his limbs stiffen in her desperate embrace. Was she alive? He gasped painfully for breath. He could not bear it. In an instant, his hands were round her throat. He was mad. All his strength flowed to his hands.

The load which had been dragging him into the water like a heavy stone fell off and he floated to the surface. Ah! Ah! He sucked in the air and longed for light and the touch of the land.

Further Reading

An Anthology of Modern Bengali Short Stories, translated by Enakshi Chatterjee (Calcutta), Prayer Books, 1977 (This includes one of Tarashankar's best-known stories, *Music Room,* which deals with the last of a line of landed aristocrats now bankrupt but anxious to recapture one last bit of splendour by organising a soirée. This story has been filmed by Satyajit Ray.)

Several novels have been translated including:

Panchgram (*Five Villages*), translated by M. Franda and S. Chatterjee (New Delhi). Manohar Book Service, 1973.

Arogyaniketan, translated by Enakshi Chatterjee (New Delhi), Arnold/Heinemann, 1977. The monograph on Bandyopadhyay in 'The Makers of Indian Literature' series is by Mahesveta Devi (New Delhi), Sahitya Akademi, 1975.

The Prize

Jainendra Kumar (1905–   )

Translated from the Hindi by Shrawan Kumar. From *Hindi Short Stories,*
edited and translated by Shrawan Kumar and Prabhakar Machwe
(Bombay), Jaico Publishing House, 1970

Jainendra Kumar, though a great admirer of Premchand and probably the
first notable Hindi writer of fiction after Premchand, was totally different
in his themes and style. His major preoccupation in his novels and stories
has been the relations between men and women which he has explored
with great skill. His novella, *Letter of Resignation,* is a *tour de force* and the
heroine's apparent fall from grace treated with an ethical outlook far more
sophisticated than one would expect from an ardent Gandhian. His style
has been criticised as being too mannered at times. In this story, however,
there is an effort to be simple since the major perspective is that of a
precocious child.

There was such a scramble at the sight of the long-awaited result
sheet that both the sheet and the *peon* bearing it might well have
been reduced to shreds, but strangely both escaped intact. The
students scanned the sheet and went away one by one. In no time
the school premises looked deserted save for a lone figure—a boy,
barely ten years old, who was still standing there, his eyes fixed on
the results.

He was Dhananjay. He had come first in his class. He walked
home briskly and triumphantly announced, I've got through,
Mum.'

His mother, busy with her domestic chores, was indifferent as
usual. His announcement, it seemed, had been lost on her.
Undaunted, he added insistently, 'Not only that Mum, I've come
first in my class. Yes, first!'

But still the mother showed no interest. An absent-minded,

'Well,' was her only reaction. She had so much to do and would suffer no distraction. Dhananjay was taken aback. Was it wrong to have come first or to have announced his pleasure? He was perplexed.

Suddenly, as if reminded of something, she said, 'Come, eat something; you went away so early without a bite or a drop of anything. You didn't listen to me and now you've returned at nine o'clock!'

'Where's Father? Has he left?'

'How do I know.'

Dhananjay felt snubbed by her answer. But to be the top of his class was no mean achievement.

'Did he leave very early today? I thought . . .' he persisted.

'Oh, as if he'd have showered prizes on you. Won't you shut up and eat something?'

Dhananjay could not imagine what could be wrong. His mother's rebuff made him go silent. He sat down quietly to the ceremony of eating but his mind was wandering far. To have stood first in his class and to be now in Class VIII at the age of ten was to him now neither an achievement nor a matter for self-satisfaction. Suddenly, sympathy welled up in his heart for his father. He could imagine how hurriedly he must have slipped into his coat and left the house, his umbrella tucked under his arm. As he munched his food, he kept thinking of the scene.

Suddenly, he was roused from his dream with a shock. His father's figure disappeared and in his place stood his wretched mother in the flesh. He froze.

'Have a little more,' she was coaxing him.

'No.'

'All right. Now don't be naughty and don't go out. Sit down over there and go over your lessons.' She pointed to the corner where his small table and chair stood gloomily.

The boy heard the command and fixed his gaze for a moment on his mother's face. But soon he lowered his eyes dutifully, collected his glass and tray and took them to their appointed place. The mother watched him at his self-assigned task for a while. The boy was fast becoming incomprehensible to her. He was unlike other boys; he looked and behaved like a grown-up and this disturbed her. She recoiled and even felt a touch of remorse. She was a mother whose motherhood did not know how to express itself. The dull affection that surged within her burst out into annoyance.

'What do you think I am? An invalid? You seem to feel very high and mighty, my dear boy, to want to do all this work by yourself but I'm not going to put up with this kind of childish nonsense.'

The boy remained silent, apparently unperturbed. He wiped his hands and face on a towel and put away the glass and tray in their rightful corner. Then he went and sat at his small table. His ease and poise proclaimed his unconcern.

This placed his mother in a difficult position. She felt deprived of a reason for letting fly at him but then he was her son and she could not possibly hurt him. Torn by an inner conflict, she sought escape in the only thing available to her—household chores and toil. Work, work, work—that was how she tried to suppress her disquiet.

In the midst of her drudgery she heard, 'I'm off.' Those two words acted as a spark on the tinder of a peace she was trying to force within her. 'No you don't,' she roared. But he, apparently oblivious to her order, was rushing towards the door. Like a flash of lightning, she leaped on him.

'How dare you? I'll beat you to a pulp!' she shrieked.

Dhananjay offered no resistance. Nor did the mother carry out her threat. She simply thrust him on to the bed and observed remonstratively, 'What do you think I am? A servant?'

'But I have to go,' the boy persisted. He was still self-composed and looked at ease as he sat on the bed, his legs dangling.

'And why, may I ask?' the woman yelled. 'Shall I teach you a lesson today?' His composure was a challenge to her.

'Mum,' said Dhananjay softly, 'Father's promised to buy sweets if I do well.'

'Your father! Sweets! He can't find a morsel of bread for the family and he's going to give you sweets! Your loving father only knows how to squander money on others. You're not going to stir out of the house.'

He looked at her in silence and she too looked back at him. She was getting confused. Naturally, she was proud of him. He was her own child and had come first among so many boys. Of course her son could not but be successful.

'Take care! If you go out you'll lose your legs!'

She had almost gone out of the room when suddenly something occurred to her and she froze at the thought. Her eyes became big as she looked questioningly at him. 'Were you going *there*? Tell me the truth,' she demanded.

This was too much for the boy and he stared at her in surprise.

'I can see it quite clearly. Perhaps it was *he* who told you to go there. . . . Well, let him come back. . . .' She was threatening.

The boy was speechless.

'Why don't you speak up? Weren't you going there with your sweets?'

'Yes,' he said and seemed to look into his mother's eyes insolently. This stunned her. Then, excited, she began beating him. She hit him incessantly for some time but he showed neither fear nor resentment. He was, in fact, the embodiment of fortitude. He did not shed a tear but suffered in silence. That only acerbated her torture.

'This is my fate,' she thought. 'No one in the house that I can call mine, except my own self and my work. And thus shall I perish. Toil is my constant companion, all else is hostile to me; perhaps only death can bring me deliverance. He goes away in the morning and expects a reception when he returns in the evening. To do and die is my lot. Frowns and chores for me; smiles and presents for someone else! And now this child, too, thinks I'm of no account, while poring over every word of *his*. This house is a prison for me—this boy chains me down. But for him I might have disappeared into the unknown, without a trace or a tear. And look at this shameless creature . . .'

Her hands were now as busy as her mind. Deftly they moved through the kitchen utensils and in a few minutes everything looked bright and orderly. The familiar rhythm of her tasks had become even more systematic today. What else could it be when her every moment was spent on improving it? To her an idle minute was like eternity, dark and abysmal.

But if her need for toil was endless, not so her routine work. It came to an end, and blankness stared her in the face. She looked into the room and found the boy sleeping soundly. She was surprised. She gazed at her son for an entire minute and softness, affection and love filled her heart. 'In my home, my own darling has to live like and orphan! I admonish and punish him without rhyme or reason. And *he* . . . he, of course, has no time for me or for my son.'

Gently she sat on the bed and held her son's head in her hands and whispered, 'My son! My dearest!'

The boy opened his eyes and for a moment wondered if it was his own mother fondling him. Yes it was, and saying loving words too! He was much affected by it and closed his eyes, giving himself up entirely to her.

Holding his face in her hands she continued to whisper endearingly, 'My darling son, what will you take as a prize from me?'

The child was overwhelmed and could not utter a word. She went on. 'Will you have two *rupees?* No, all right then, have five. . . .'

'Oh, how nice! Fondling her son!' She heard someone call out from the staircase. It was *he,* her husband, the child's father. He walked into the room, hung his umbrella on the peg and began unbuttoning his coat.

She got up. Her face was again tense. With tight lips she made for the door but the boy got up quickly and announced with urgent anticipation his examination success.

'So, that's what made her offer you a prize of five rupees!'

'What five rupees? Who's offered him five rupees? As if you've showered wealth on me. I'm here just to slave while your money's for someone else.'

The complaint in her torrent of words was not lost on Dhananjay's father but he did not answer back. He did not want to make matters worse. He spoke to his son instead.' Tell me what shall I get for you? Come let's decide.'

The boy thought for a while and then wanted to make sure that the offer still stood. 'Of course. You deserve it. It was no joke beating a hundred other boys.'

'Let me have my money back, Dhani,' his mother broke in and

snatched the five rupee note from him. Unwilling to stay even a second in her husband's presence she dashed off to the kitchen.

Someone's footsteps were heard on the stairs. She could tell whose they were by the sound. They were Pramila's. Her whole attention was riveted on the newcomer. Pramila came in carrying a plate covered with a cloth. Dhananjay's mother would not even look at that female creature, much less at her obvious pleasure, her smiling face and sparkling eyes. But she could not help stealing a glance.

'This is for you, my love,' Pramila said to Dhananjay,' but just you wait. What a naughty boy! Topping the list and not telling anybody!'

The mother was listening to every word. A shudder ran through her when she heard her husband softly utter the woman's name— 'Pramila.' Her eyes slyly followed the two of them through a chink in the kitchen window. Pramila had embraced the boy but the mother noticed that he was trying to free himself from her arms. With a side-glance at the kitchen, the boy also noticed his mother's look of despair.

Pramila removed the cloth from the plate and urged Dhananjay to ask for whatever he wanted on such a joyful occasion.

'Do you mean that?' the child asked with a rare intensity.

'Of course. Only don't ask for me you little rascal.'

'Never. It's something else. But you won't go back on your promise?'

'Foolish child, why should I?'

The boy drew Pramila to his side and made her sit by him. He put his arm round her and said with much tenderness, 'Please, no excuses. I know you love me very much but promise me you won't visit us any more.'

'What nonsense!' shouted the father, but the child was equal to it. Back came his request with added emphasis. 'You, too, Father, made a promise to give me something. You'll have to honour your promise, sir. You shan't meet her in future.'

His father and Pramila were flabbergasted. His mother, who had heard it all, was overwhelmed. She rushed in and took the boy in her arms. Turning to her husband she implored, 'What are you looking at? Why be mean? Part with that ten-rupee note quickly and let's all enjoy ourselves together.'

To Pramila who was stunned she said, 'Pramila, dear, it's been a long time since you visited us last. Let's celebrate together.'

It was the finest moment Dhananjay had known. Yes, only a moment perhaps, but couldn't a moment last for ever?

Further Reading

Hardly any of Jainendra's stories or novels have been translated into English.

Jahnavi, a story about a girl who questions traditional morality, is to be found in *Contemporary Indian Short Stories Vol. II* (New Delhi) Sahitya Akademi, 2nd ed 1977

Tyagpatra (Letter of Resignation), a short novel, translated by S. Saksena (Benares), The India Library, 1948, is considered by many to be his masterpiece.

The New Constitution

Saadat Hasan Manto (1911–1955)

Translated from the Urdu by Hamid Jalal. From *Nothing But The Truth: Pakistani Short Stories,* edited by Faruq Hassan and Khalid Hassan (Montreal), Dawson College, 1978

Almost forgotten today and his works out of print, Manto was regarded in his lifetime as one of the foremost Urdu short-story writers. Along with a bevy of literary stars all of whom shone in this particular genre—people like Krishan Chander, Bedi, Chugtai, Ghulam Abbas—he wrote about the common man and woman and the down-and-out in the slums of the city.

Manto's native city of Lahore is the setting for this story. The events take place on the eve of the implementation of the 1935 Government of India Act which was to provide a measure of autonomy under British rule. Though Manto's life was short and full of stress, it did not prevent him from writing about the richness of life. The characters he created, like Ustad Mangu, the hero of this story, are typically forceful and vigorous. The story is very nationalistic in tone and contains references to the politics of the day—the Spanish Civil War, Mussolini and the Bolshevik Revolution in Russia.

At the *tonga* stand near the railway station, Mangu enjoyed the reputation of being a wise man. All the other tonga drivers who used that stand regarded him as their mentor and called him *ustad*. In bestowing this professional title on Mangu, they had not taken into account the fact that he had never attended any school, even for a day, but his illiteracy was no bar to his keen interest in world affairs. Whenever any tonga driver wanted to know what was going on in the world, he would always draw on Ustad Mangu's fund of topical knowledge.

Some time back, Mangu had overheard some of his passengers discussing rumours of a war in Spain. On his return to the stand, he had slapped Gama Chaudhry on his broad back and, with a grave expression on his face, had predicted, 'Mark my words, Chaudhry, war's in the offing in Spain!' Gama Chaudhry had asked where Spain was and Ustad Mangu had replied with great confidence that it was near England, where else?

When war did break out in Spain, the tonga drivers at the railway stand, squatting in a circle and smoking *hookahs,* were full of admiration for Mangu's political foresight. At that time Mangu was plying his tonga on the glistening tarmac of the Mall, exchanging views with his fare on the latest Hindu-Muslim riots. When he returned to the stand that evening, his face showed signs of animation. With the hookah going around someone mentioned the Hindu-Muslim clashes. He took off his khaki turban, tucked it under his arm and spoke in sombre tones: 'I tell you, the curse of some *pir* is on us. That's why the Hindus and Muslims are at each other's throats every other day. I've heard the elders say that Akbar Badshah★ had displeased a *dervesh* who then put a curse on his kingdom saying that there would always be strife in his Hindustan and that's what has been happening ever since.' He paused, heaved a sigh, puffed his hookah and continued, 'These Congresswalas★ want Hindustan to be free but I say they'll get nowhere even if they keep at it for a thousand years. The most that can happen is the Angrez★ will go away and the Itlywala★ or the Rooswala★ will come in. Hindustan will remain enslaved forever and, I forgot to tell you, that pir also said that Hindustan will always be ruled by foreigners.'

Ustad Mangu hated the British because, as he explained, they held his country in subjugation and had perpetrated countless atrocities on his countrymen. But he despised them most because of his ill-treatment at the hands of British soldiers in the cantonment. They treated him as if he were a dog. He also had an aversion for their complexion—their pink and ruddy faces made him feel sick; why, he could never understand. He said that their faces reminded him of a corpse whose skin was peeling off. Whenever he had a quarrel with some drunken tommy,★ Ustad Mangu would feel very upset for days after the incident. At the stand in the evening he would curse the man. He would shake his head, swathed loosely in his turban, and say, 'They came for a light and stayed on as masters of the house! I'm fed up with these sons of monkeys. They order us about as if we were servants in their father's house.'

He would not cool down easily. As long as there was a companion by his side he would go on unburdening himself. 'Oh! What a sight he was, like carrion. He wouldn't have survived a slap . . . went on saying something like "git-pit" as if he was about to kill me. I thought of knocking his head off but controlled myself with the thought that it would be below my dignity.' He would pause, wipe his nose on the sleeve of his khaki shirt, and start grumbling. 'By God, I'm absolutely fed up with being nice and polite to these *lat sahibs*. Whenever I see their ill-fated faces, my blood starts to boil. I wish we had some more rights under a new constitution or something so that we'd be saved from them. I swear by your life that things would be all right then!'

Then, one day, he overheard two persons whom he had picked up from the district courts saying that a new constitution was shortly to be enforced. His face lit up and his joy knew no bounds.

The new constitutional reforms for India were being discussed by the two Marwari* passengers who had gone to court over some civil case. 'I've heard that the new India Act will come into force from the first of April. Will everything change with its enactment?'

'Not everything, but I've heard that a lot of things will change and that Hindustan will get independence.'

'Will the new constitution make any change in the laws regulating money-lending?'

'I'm not sure. We'll ask the lawyer.'

This conversation filled Ustad Mangu with immense happiness. He was always rather rough with his horse; besides showering it with abuse, he would use his whip freely. But today, as he looked back every now and then at the Marwaris, he flicked his big moustache with his finger, let the reins drop loose on the horse's back and said very affectionately, 'Come on, my son, let's fly with the wind.'

After dropping the Marwaris at their destination, he went to Dinu *halwai's** shop in Anarkarli and drank almost two pints of *lassi*. He belched loudly and appreciatively, sucked the dripping ends of his moustache and suddenly shouted, 'Oh you so and so's!'

When he returned to the stand that evening, he did not find any of his cronies there. This unusual situation caused a strange turmoil in his mind. Today he had big news for his friends, very big news, but none of them was there. He did not know how to get it off his chest. For half an hour he walked up and down under the corrugated-iron shed of the tonga stand, his whip tucked under his arm, each step betraying his impatience. He was feeling elated and his mind was full of rosy pictures. News of the new constitution had transported him to a new world and he was examining, from every possible angle, the India Act which was to be enforced from the first of April.

The Marwaris had been worried about the effect of the new laws on usury. This delighted him. The ends of his big moustache quivered as he laughed and cursed the Marwaris. 'You bugs in the poor man's cot! The new constitution will be like boiling water for the likes of you.'

He was especially happy when he thought how the new constitution would affect the tommies—those white mice, as he called them—would scamper into their holes forever.

When his friend, Nathu, entered the stand, his bald head shining, Ustad Mangu almost leapt at him shouting, 'Here, give me your hand. I'll give you news that'll make you so happy that hair will start growing again on your bald pate.'

Ustad Mangu had heard a great deal about the socialist system of the Soviet Union and had been much impressed by its new constitution and other experiments. He had mixed up Rooswala Badshah* with the India Act and thought that the changes that were to come into effect were due to the influence of the Russian King.

For some time the Red Shirt movement* had been quite active in Peshawar and some other towns. He had also mixed up this organisation with the Russians and the old constitution. Whenever he heard of people being arrested for making bombs or on a charge of rebellion he thought they were the forerunners of the new order of things and he felt very optimistic about the future.

One day, two barristers in his tonga were criticising the new constitution. He heard them in silence. One of them was saying,

'The second part of the constitution envisages a federation. I've not been able to understand it. It's unlike any other federation in history. In fact, it's no federation at all'

As the barristers had used a large number of English words Mangu could follow only the opening and he got the impression they were opposed to the new act which in his mind was nothing short of treason. He could not conceive of anyone opposing his own country's freedom. He looked at them full of contempt and muttered, 'Toadies!'

Whenever he heard this word, 'toady', he would feel gratified at the thought that he had used it correctly and that he could distinguish between a man of honour and a 'toady'.

Three days after that incident, he overheard three students from Government College discussing the same subject as he drove them to Mozang. One of them said, 'The new constitution has filled me with high hopes. If that friend of mine gets elected to the Assembly, I can be sure of a job in some government office.' Another said, 'There should be a lot of new posts and a big drop in the number of unemployed graduates.'

Their talk made Ustad Mangu even more enthusiastic and he came to regard the new constitution as the radiant path to a new era. He compared it to the new harness he had bought for his horse two years ago from Chaudhry Khuda Buksh. He had selected the material very carefully. Its nickel-plated buttons, brass fittings and other trappings had glistened and shone under the sun. The new constitution, too, had to be something that would scintillate and dazzle and give a new colour and light to all things drab and dull.

Before the first of April he heard a great deal for and against the new constitution. But nothing changed the picture in his mind. He was sure that on the first of April every dark cloud would lift, the atmosphere would be radiant and the world bathed in a cool, soothing light.

At last, the thirty-one days of March were over and all that remained were a few hours of the last night of the month. The weather was unusually cool for the time of the year and the breeze had a pleasing fragrance about it. Early on the morning of the first of April, Ustad Mangu went to the stable and harnessed his horse between the tonga shafts. In the thin haze of the early morning, he drove his tonga through several bazaars and wide roads but nothing had changed. Everything was old, as old as the sky. His eyes searched for new colours and shapes but the only new object was the bunch of multi-coloured feathers on the head of his horse. He had brought this new headgear for fourteen and a half *annas* for the new day.

The tramp of his horse, the evenly-spaced lamp posts on the side of the road, the shop signs, the little bells jingling round the horse's neck, the people in the bazaars. What was new in all this? But he did not lose heart. When he reached Government College, the clock in the tower was striking nine. The students were dressed well enough but to him they looked shabby. Where were the gay, bright colours symbolic of the day?

He turned left into Anarkali. Shops were starting to open and traffic picking up. The confectioners' shops were crowded, the general merchants' windows full of new attractions and on the telegraph wires several pigeons were pecking at each other. But nothing interested Ustad Mangu. He wanted to see some concrete manifestation of the new constitution, as tangible as his horse.

For Ustad Mangu it had always been difficult to live through periods of expectancy. He had become a nervous wreck during the last four or five months of his wife's pregnancy. He knew the baby would take its own time but he had never had any patience with the clock. If only he could have had a brief glimpse of his child, the baby could be born whenever it desired. To fulfil this impossible wish of his, he had several times felt the swollen stomach of his ailing wife and even put his ear to it but had got no clue as to what the baby would look like. Once he had lost all restraint and shouted at his wife. 'Why are you always in bed as if you were dead? Get up, take some exercise or you'll never have strength for the delivery. Lying flat on your back is no way to have babies.'

Ustad Mangu wanted to see quick results. His wife would say, 'You're thirsty even before the well's been bored.' But he was not as impatient as usual about the new constitution. Today he had set out to see its effects just as he used to come out to see the processions when Gandhi and Nehru came to the city. He always judged the popularity and prestige of leaders from the size and noise of their processions and the weight of the garlands round their necks. The deeper the leader was submerged in flowers, the bigger he became in Mangu's eyes; and if there was any disturbance and police action during the procession, the leader's prestige went up even higher. Now he wanted to weigh the new constitution on the same scales.

He had come out of Anarkali and was driving the tonga slowly down the Mall when he was hailed by a man who wanted to go to the cantonment. 'That's good,' he thought. 'I'll see some signs of the new constitution there.' When he had dropped the passenger off and was holding a cigarette between the third and fourth fingers of his left hand, settled comfortably on the cushioned back seat, his horse cantering very slowly along the road, Mangu let his thoughts saunter lazily over the new constitution. What, he wondered, would its rules be about getting tonga licences from the city authorities? He was sure that it would remove the present difficulties. Suddenly, he became aware that someone was calling out, wanting to hire his tonga. It was a tommy standing near a lamp post.

When he saw the tommy all his hatred of British soldiers welled up and he thought of ignoring the man. Then he reasoned with himself. It would be foolishness not to take their money. The fourteen and a half annas he had spent on the plume should come from the tommy's pocket.

He turned the tonga neatly on the empty road and asked the soldier in a sarcastic tone, '*Sahib bahadur,* where do you want to go?' His moustache-covered lip curled up contemptuously and the faint wrinkle which ran down his cheek from his nostril to his chin, suddenly became prominent as if someone had etched a line on brown *sheeshum* wood with a sharp knife.

The soldier who was trying to light a cigarette, shielding himself from the breeze, turned towards the tonga and saw Ustad Mangu. It seemed as if two guns, pointing at each other, had gone off and were disintegrating in the explosion. Ustad Mangu unwound his reins from his left hand as he prepared to step down from the tonga. He was glaring at the tommy as if he were going to chew him up. The tommy, too, was flicking off imaginary specks from his blue trousers, nervously awaiting Ustad Mangu's onslaught. He blew some cigarette smoke and said, 'Do you want to go or are you going to make trouble again?'

'It's the same one,' and the unspoken words began to dance about in Mangu's broad chest. It was the same tommy with whom he had had an altercation the previous year. The soldier had been drunk and Ustad Mangu had had to bear a lot of abuse from him. He could have knocked him down, given him a good hiding but had thought it wiser to exercise self-control for he knew that magistrates took a severe view of tonga drivers who beat up British tommies.

'Where do you want to go?' He spoke as if he were lashing the tommy with his whip.

'To the red light district,' the soldier said.

'That'll cost you five rupees.'

'Five rupees?' the tommy shouted indignantly. 'Are you out of your mind?'

'Yes, five rupees.' Mangu clenched his big hairy hand and started examining his fist. 'Do you want to go or are you going to waste my time?'

His tone was harsh. In the light of last year's incident, the tommy did not take Ustad Mangu's towering build into account. He thought that the tonga driver should again be taught a lesson. So he strutted up to the tonga and signalling with his stick told Mangu to step down. The polished stick touched Mangu's thigh twice. From his perch he sized up the soldier who was of medium height and build. Then his fist shot out and landed on the tip of the soldier's chin. Mangu clambered out of his seat and pushed the tommy back and was soon giving him the thrashing of his life. The man tried his best to ward off the heavy blows but when he saw that his opponent was fighting like a maniac, his eyes bloodshot, he began to yell for help. This spurred on Ustad Mangu and the ferocity of his attack increased. He hit the tommy again and again and every time he landed a blow he would say, 'Still that high and mighty tone! It's the first of April and now we are our own masters.'

A crowd collected. It was with great difficulty that two policemen managed to restrain Mangu. He stood between them, his broad chest heaving as he panted for breath. He was foaming at the mouth but his eyes were smiling. Struggling for breath, he addressed the amazed crowd. 'Gone are the days of the British. We now have a new constitution, brothers, a new constitution.'

The poor tommy touched his badly hurt face and looked owlishly at the people.

The constable took Ustad Mangu to the police station. On the way he kept shouting, 'The new constitution! The new constitution!' But no one understood what he meant.

'What are you screaming about?' the sergeant snarled. 'What new constitution? What new laws? It's the same old law, brother.'

And Ustad Mangu was duly locked up in a cell.

Further Reading

The only translations of Manto's short stories appeared shortly after his death in a volume entitled, *Black Milk*, translated by Hamid Jalal. Some of them have been reprinted in:
Nothing but the Truth: Pakistani Short Stories, ed. Faruq Hassan and Khalid Hassan (Montreal), Dawson College, 1978

The Leader

Abu Jafar Shamsuddin (1911–   )

Translated from the Bengali by Ranjana Ash. Taken from the author's collection called *Shreshta Galpa* (Dacca) 1967

The famous Bangladeshi writer, Abu Jafar Shamsuddin, began his writing career as a journalist in undivided Bengal in 1930 but soon combined his journalism with literature.

This is a story about the hollowness of a silver-tongued political orator whose socialism turns out to be little more than bombast when confronted with the enormity of the Bengal Famine when some four million people perished. This was not a famine due to natural causes but to wartime bungling, profiteering and political negligence. To depict the significance of the holocaust through a few powerful similes and metaphors is an effective literary device and the effect is enhanced by the contrast between the two styles—the bland irony to describe the political posturing of the radicals and the very eloborate imagery for the victims of the holocaust.

The political group with which I was involved suffered from a lack of speakers so that after I had delivered a few speeches I found I had become a sort of minor leader. I cannot remember the kind of speeches I used to make but what I do recall quite clearly is the applause which would be showered on me like nectar from the gods at the end of my peroration as I came down from the platform. Even I began to be surprised by my ability and regretted not having exploited such a talent earlier in life. I reproached myself for having concealed it from public view in order to earn a living, otherwise my name, too, would have been blazoned in letters of gold along with our national leaders. If only I had thrown in my lot with some well-established political organisation there would have been no end to my success. I might even have become a minister or governor by now. When I spoke at a party rally, the audience, without exception, would listen in pin-drop silence. I noticed that comrade Debika's sister, Tara, had begun to gaze at me though I, being a mere speech-maker and no poet, could not possibly probe the language of that look. This much I could tell, however, was that it was full of meaning, conveying possibly respect and perhaps even love.

I had never known a woman's love nor experienced the bliss such love brings, but I had the normal quota of curiosity and eagerness. Inevitably I was drawn to Tara and used to love to talk to her on the slightest pretext. She was full of respect which was natural as she had only just passed her matriculation examination. In spite of the awe she appeared to have, a kind of intimacy began to blossom between us and I became more involved with Debika's work than before.

Debika was a well-known political figure. She had been connected with almost every revolutionary movement at some stage of her life and her reputation had spread throughout Bengal. When I got to know her, she had lost her earlier faith in the Terrorist Movement* and ideology. She had learnt the hard way that the ideals she stood for required the co-operation, support and active involvement of the mass of the people. No sooner had this truth dawned on her than she began going from village to village seeking support for her party. She would walk mile upon mile along village tracks of dust and mud.

The Famine of 1943 had started and to talk to the people about the need for a united front to win the war against fascism seemed ludicrous. Still Debika worked tirelessly at it. She took her politics to the weak and emaciated villagers, to the market place and to the docks. Indeed, she invited me to speak at one of her meetings. She said that Tara, too, would be coming and that Tara was now showing quite a lot of interest in politics. Debika was going to speak and so must I.

I was thrilled to hear that Tara would be going with us. The meeting was to be in a distant village and it would not be possible to return the same day so undoubtedly we would have a lot of time together without any interruption. Such a golden opportunity might never come again so I was ready to go as soon as asked. But, as one should never make oneself too accessible, I went through the usual formalities before accepting: was it very far, would we have accommodation for the night and would there be a reasonable audience? She reassured me on all these points and said that she was hoping for a large turn-out. 'They've had drummers,' she said, 'at every market square to tell the people. Everyone knows it's going to be about the food problem so there's bound to be a crowd.'

To have not only the certainty of being with Tara for the next twenty-four hours but also the prospect of a large audience increased my enthusiasm, but I said with the right note of moderate concern, 'Very well. Since you're so keen I might as well go.'

The next day I went to Goriahat Road to wait for them. Tara was standing on her sister's right. The simple attire she had chosen for the occasion suited her. Debika was overjoyed on seeing me. 'Come along, comrade, come along. The bus will be leaving in five minutes.' Without a word I went and stood next to Tara. I wondered whether I could ever surmount the insurmountable and break down the social barriers and taboos between us and make Tara my life's companion.

The market place of Gundugram village was as miserable in appearance as it was impoverished in reality. A few small thatched huts stood in the middle, like widowed women shorn of all their ornaments. Not one had a fence. The only shop, as such, was the village grocer's.

It was almost five o'clock by the time we had walked the three miles from the bus stop down the winding footpaths across the fields. People were gathering for the meeting. I had started to speak and was pontificating on national and international issues in a loud voice and, every now and then, denouncing the fascist powers. Of course I also included the tyranny of British imperialism; there was the occasional applause. Suddenly, I saw a strange sight. I was speaking from a high platform and could see into the distance. Almost half a mile away, a host of people were advancing toward us. As they came closer their forms became clearer. They were women. In tattered clothes covered with dust, they leaned forward as they walked. The wind blew against them and as they could not stand up to the force of the wind, they leaned forward like hunchbacks. Some seemed to have their heads touching the ground in front of them. Their hair, long deprived of oil, was dust-covered and matted. As no sari covered their heads, their hair was blowing about wildly like falling leaves. Their ragged clothes were flying around. The outline of their ribs stood out from their dark, copper-coloured bodies. Their stomachs seemed to have merged with their backs. Women's breasts—cups that contain nectar—were shrivelled and hanging like bats or like the torn pockets of a shirt. Some of the women had children in their arms or on their backs.

As they moved it seemed as if a nest of snakes were crawling in a zigzag course. In their eyes and faces was the savage look of hunger. They were like sudden and unexpected storm clouds from a northern land that were rushing forward at an incredible speed to devour the earth. They were in all shades of black: angry black, horrific black, pitch black, grey-black—ominous black banks of clouds ranged in columns in the sky surging to devour the entire human race to satisfy their perennial hunger.

Still they advanced. It seemed as if their long arms had become separated from the rest of their bodies and were dangling with slight support as when a branch is lopped off a mighty tree and hangs from the bark. Their arms hung like a skeleton's—the fingers as long as iron nails. Their eyes, sunk into deep hollows, were the fearful eyes of some reptile. Like the serried teeth of a crocodile, their teeth were exposed as if they had been pushed out of their jaws.

They were like some subterranean legendary monsters which had not been able to satisfy their hunger despite cutting through rocks and mountains with their razor-edged tongues and had been forced to emerge into the open. Trees, vines, leaves, animals, birds, insects, mankind—everything on land, sea and air—would be devoured by them and only then would their hunger be appeased. Just as the deluge rises out of the raging sea and engulfs everything in its path, so these creatures would swallow all that fell before them. There would be neither pity nor anger, no mercy or envy, no thought. Humanity would be left with nothing. Dancing a dance of destruction, like Shiva's *tandav*★they would consume the entire world with the supreme indifference of cold-blooded creatures.

Like the lizard on the wall that swallows flies and gnats with a flick of its tongue, their voracious hunger would spare neither you, me nor anyone else.

I cannot remember when my speech ended but I stayed on the platform staring in front, every nerve in my body tingling, as if held by a very powerful magnet. As the snake's victim is immobilised by the predator's hypnotic gaze and awaits its end in the killer's maws, so I awaited my fate at the hands of this army of human reptiles. They came nearer and nearer to the very edge of the field: bony hands of skeletons from hell spread out in front of me—tentacles, ready to coil round their prey and imprison it in their powerful net; giant crabs opening their long pincers to ensnare their food. Some sinister magic had breathed life into the dead from the nether world to consume human civilisation.

Suddenly, the skeletons, possessed by demons, screamed in unison, 'We want food! We want rice! We want corn!' It was the screeching of canes in a bamboo grove as they split in the wind. Their screams broke my spell. Yelling wildly, I jumped off the platform and ran breathlessly down the rural district board's red pebbled path. Escape was vital to life. I did not dare look back. I kept on hearing their cries: 'We want food! We want rice! We want corn!' piercing my eardrums. My heart thumped like a hammer as I ran faster, oblivious to anybody else. How to save my own skin was my sole preoccupation as I fled. As I was the leader, the star speaker, they were bound to pursue me and devour me. I ran even faster. I was the leader with a future and I must survive for the sake of that future. These living skeletons, possessed by the devil, would be on earth for only a little while and then vanish but I would once again be in the midst of good times and plenty. So I had to save myself from their onslaught. I must escape and with this determination I began to race with greater energy. But running away then or since will never erase the horrific memory.

Further Reading

Unfortunately, none of Shamshuddin's works are available in English. One hopes that his *magnum opus, Padma Meghna, Jamuna,* an epic of some 1,200 pages dealing with life in East Bengal from the time of the First World War to the emergence of Bangladesh, will be translated. It is one of the best chronicles of Bengali Muslim life and of the forces that led to the creation of Pakistan and, in turn, Bangladesh.

The Jagirdar and his Dog

Pannalal Patel (1912–   )

Translated from the Gujerati by Dhananjay Desai. From *Modern Indian Short Stories,* Vol. II (New Delhi), Indian Council for Cultural Relations, 1976

Though a relatively recent genre in Gujerati writing, the short story has become popular. Patel is one of a trio of what might be called the middle generation of writers after pioneers like Dhumketu, Meghani and Joshi. Along with Broker and Madia he became well known in the 1940s. Whereas Broker deals mainly with Gujerati middle-class characters, Madia and Patel are more at home in a rural setting. Madia's powerfully symbolic story, *The Earning Son,* reveals the conflict between the rural classes and castes through the symbol of a stud-ox and ends on a very violent note.

In this story the theme of feudal snobbery, arrogance and autocracy is shown through the antics of a petty aristocrat—the Jagirdar—and his pampered dog. The so-called independent states of pre-Independence India with their princes and other ranks of the nobility sided with the British *raj* not only politically but culturally. The story makes fun of the Jagirdar's aping of the British way of life while showing his rudeness to his social inferiors. The violent ending is typical of many South Asian stories which begin comically but cannot ignore social and economic reality.

After his return from England, the Jagirdar★ was visiting our village for the first time and everybody was awaiting his arrival. The Talati★ had started keeping the milk-pot ready for almost a week. Who could say when Bapu★ would suddenly appear. Cots and bedding were collected and the village headman was instructed not to leave the village. The barber, cobbler and water-carrier were ordered to be ready to serve Bapu at a moment's notice. A few policemen were on round-the-clock duty and had to leave substitutes when they went home for meals. Then the Jagirdar's personal cook, domestic servants and bodyguards arrived early one morning and a wave of suspense spread throughout the village. The cook took charge of the kitchen with four men from the village to assist him. The headman was busy the whole time helping with the Jagirdar's entourage. The policemen got the utensils, milk and curds from the villagers while other culinary ingredients were purchased from the village grocer's shop. Of course, the entire village would have to bear the cost of entertaining the Jagirdar.

The Talati, wearing a jacket and breeches, stitched by the village tailor about five years ago, and a pink turban, scurried about impatiently, keeping an eye on the road. Somebody said, 'I can hear a car,' and soon a huge crowd had gathered where the road turned. 'There it comes. See that dust rising. It'll be here in no time.' The policemen rushed in front. 'Fools! Get out of the way. Fall into line, you rascals, and don't you make a noise when Bapu comes. You idiot, over there, bow down to him respectfully.'

Bapu's car arrived, raising dust over the bowed heads of the villagers, and stopped near the village square. The door opened and Bapu stepped out, followed by a snow-white creature with long ears, short legs and a lot of fur all over its body. Bapu's secretary got out last from the back seat.

The Jagirdar was a young man of about twenty-eight. He was not particularly handsome but he was well-built and dressed in great style—trousers, jacket, tie, socks, shoes, wristwatch and a beautiful ring. He had a stick in one hand and a chain-like thing in the other. He looked as if he had come straight from the ship that had brought him back from England. But nobody paid any attention to him even while bowing low to pay their respects to him. They were looking at the strange little animal near his feet.

When they talked among themselves later, they could only wonder about the animal's ancestry. Was it an English rabbit or a British panther? Some knew it was neither a dog nor a cat but could not decide its species. The conjectures spread and bets were placed while a few were really scared. 'I wish Bapu would keep the creature chained. It might kill somebody.' Some young men were sure it was a dog but they could not figure out its name which varied from Shivler to Filoo. They waxed eloquent about the dog's wonderful ears that were so long that they seemed to touch the ground, and its short legs. But it was its hair which excited them.

'Just like a *sadhu's* matted locks,' said one, and another thought the gleaming white might be real silver. He had heard that English ladies had golden hair so perhaps their dogs had silver fur. 'You never can tell. In a country like England anything's possible.' Everybody laughed over it and concurred that Bapu was not the sort of man to bring back an ordinary dog.

The whole village kept on talking about the dog and a few even made fun of it. The headman reminded them not to say silly things, as Bapu was fonder of the dog than his own son. 'It's not a mere dog: it's Bapu's dog.' Hundreds of eyes followed the dog trotting behind its master. When Bapu sat on a cot, the dog clambered up as well. When Bapu said something that sounded like 'Silaun' it would sit down quietly. People were amazed. Was 'Silaun' its name or some special kind of command? They realised that the dog was to be respected more than the Jagirdar's secretary and even more than his son. For when the Jagirdar had come to the village three years before his own son had not dared to jump on the cot with such freedom.

Its name was Siloo—from silver—and the villagers started calling it Siloobhai. They were astounded when they knew the dog had cost five hundred rupees. One could buy twenty bullocks or five horses with that amount. Siloobhai was as expensive as an elephant and cost its weight in silver.

But the dogs of the village were not so respectful. As soon as they saw Siloo, they started to bark as if he were another stray dog and Siloo responded by producing a bark which the villagers compared to a tiger's roar! 'Don't be silly!' one young man protested. 'Let it fight our village dogs and I bet that in no time at all it'll be licked.'

But the villagers were not convinced. They wanted Bapu to let Siloo loose so that it might show the timid village dogs its strength. Some went to Janu Mian who was in charge of looking after Siloo and begged him to let Siloobhai come out just once and make the village dogs take to their heels. It would be such fun.

The Jagirdar shouted at them. 'Damn fools, what are you staring at? Drive away those bloody *pariahs*.' Soon everybody began chasing the dogs away with stones. They ran off. The sound of their barking echoed down the streets but the moment the villagers turned their backs, the dogs reappeared joined by their friends from some other part of the village. Within ten minutes the situation had become tense and the headman had to go to the Jagirdar with the people's request. 'Bapu, why not let Siloobhai free just once? These dogs won't dare to stay anywhere near.'

'Oh no, once it gets excited, it'll be impossible to control it. Here it can be kept under my control,' the Jagirdar said, twirling his moustache.

'Of course that's quite right, such a very obedient dog,' remarked the headman. But an old man with an impudent smile wanted to know if the dog could take on a tiger. Another tried to correct his friend. 'You mean Siloobhai, don't you. Why a cheetah would jump into a ravine at the very sight of Siloobhai.'

The Jagirdar tied a chain round Siloo's neck as the dog was getting impatient to show off its skill. The headman arrived with a cup of tea. Bapu was about to take it when he demanded. 'Don't you have anything like a table?' The man was confused. He had seen something in a hotel when he had visited the Jagirdar's capital. 'You mean a chair, don't you?'

'You idiot, why should I want a chair. I want to put this cup down.' The villagers who had been listening somewhat perplexed now ran in all directions to find a table. But what could they bring? A basket placed upside down would be too low. What about a drum? So three of them rushed off to fetch a drum. As the cup was about to be put on the drum, the Jagirdar shouted at them, 'Are you all stupid or what? At least wipe the dust off.' They began to dust it vigorously and a young man beat the drum so hard with his shoulder cloth that all the dust began to fall on the dog which annoyed the Jagirdar even more.

'Idiot!' he called out.

'May I clean Siloobhai?'

Bapu sneered. 'What for? To clean your shoulder cloth?'

They did not know what to say when the impudent old man came to their rescue. 'Siloobhai is whiter than your cloth.' They began to laugh except for the young man who felt slighted. 'It may be as white as snow but it's still a dog.'

The village headman wanted to change the subject. 'What shall I do about Siloobhai's tea, Bapu?'

'Why, don't you have any more tea?' The Jagirdar's voice was stern.

Quickly tea was brought for the dog and they were curious to see how the white man's dog would drink tea. Somebody said they should bring another drum and put the dog's cup on it. 'Ass!' shouted Bapu. 'It's not going to drink from a cup. Where the devil are my servants?'

All the servants and the policemen, drinking steaming-hot tea inside, were in a panic. But before they could rush out, it had all been arranged. A rug was spread on the floor for Siloobhai and tea brought in a brass bowl. The villagers lost interest. Their dogs had it the same way.

The local dogs were getting excited again. Taking advantage of everybody's attention being on Siloobhai drinking tea, they ventured closer. The Jagirdar told his dog to sit and finish its tea. 'Then you can do whatever you like.'

The villagers were looking forward to a fight and were not going to chase their dogs away. Finally, Bapu came out with Siloo and the chain round the dog's neck flashed like silver in the sun. He screamed at the villagers, 'Don't stand in the way, idiots. Go, on, Siloo!"

Siloo growled and rushed at the striped dog which seemed to retreat. The Jagirdar taunted, 'Running away? Come forward.' But the striped dog was clever enough not to advance at an inopportune moment. It bided its time. Suddenly, someone screamed, 'Bapu, look out!' But a black dog had already bitten Bapu on the foot. During the commotion that followed, Siloo broke loose from Bapu's hand. The villagers were agitated. Some examined the injured foot while others ran to rescue Siloo who was now being attacked from all sides. They could hear its piteous cries but could not see it anywhere. They were throwing stones at their dogs and beating them with sticks when the Jagirdar screamed, 'Bring my gun, you fools.' But before the gun arrived, Siloo lay convulsed with pain in a pool of blood. Its blue eyes were more frightening than Bapu's gun and even more fearful were the cries of the dying dog. People could not bear the hideous sight and drifted home.

'Idiots! What are you all staring at? Go and bring all the dogs to that lane and then make yourselves scarce. If you don't do this, in spite of my warning, I won't be responsible for the consequences.'

They all thought it better to leave, and in a few minutes the place was deserted except for the Jagirdar. Most of the villagers remained in their homes. Even those who could not escape from the clutches of the Jagirdar's servants and the police tried their best to hide their dogs. In fact, the Jagirdar's men were rather reluctant to do the job but there was no other way to appease the Jagirdar. They told the villagers to get hold of a few dogs and that would save the village further trouble.

They found about ten dogs but only half of them were taken to the lane where the Jagirdar was waiting to shoot them. He finished them off and shouted for the rest. Nobody dared answer. Janu Mian mustered up courage to say that they could not be found. They must have left the village.

'Nonsense! These rascals must have hidden them in their houses. Go and search them and when you find them bring the master of the house along with his dog.' But then he changed his mind. 'Never mind. You people are all good-for-nothings. Go and cover Siloo up and put him in my car.'

Janu Mian could not find a piece of cloth except the young man's shoulder cloth which had been considered too dirty to clean the living Siloo only an hour ago. The young man wondered what wrong he could have done that he must be stripped of his *pachhedi*. He kept on asking himself the same question as the Jagirdar's car drove out of the village. All the villagers knew that each of them would have to contribute his share to pay for the Jagirdar's loss but at that moment they could only feel relief that their Bapu and his entourage had gone.

The street looked gruesome. There was silence everywhere save for the whirr of the crows' wings and the dying moans of the dogs. Then the village *Bhangi* arrived and he had to stroll about like a ghost in a graveyard waiting for the animals to die.

Further Reading

Very few Gujerati writers have been translated into English. *Modern Indian Short Stories,* Vol. II (New Delhi), Indian Council for Cultural Relations, 1976, contains a few stories by well-known writers such as Gulabdas Broker and Chandrakant Bakshi. One of the most outstanding stories by a Gujerati writer is *The Earning Son* by Chunilal K. Madia and it can be found in:

Contemporary Indian Short Stories, Vol. II (New Delhi), Sahitya Akademi, 2nd ed., 1977.

A Blind Man's Contentment

Thakazhi Sivasankara Pillai (1914–   )

Translated from the Malayalam by V. Abdulla. From *Malayalam Short Stories,* by Trichur Kerala, Sahitya Akademi, 1976

The only story in this anthology from the four major literatures of southern India—Tamil, Telegu, Kannada and Malayalam—is by one of the foremost writers of the subcontinent. Thakazhi Pillai's novels are famous for their depiction of the most down-trodden sections of Kerala society—the 'untouchable' farm labourers, the fisherfolk, the slum-dwellers of the city.

Pillai first made his mark as a writer of short stories. A disciple of A. Balakrishna Pillai—the father of modern progressive literature in Kerala— he followed his mentor's revolutionary ideals to develop into one of the greatest Malayali writers. His social realism is not just mere documentation but is full of passion and deep insight.

The hero of the present tale, Pappu Nayar, is from a high caste while his wife is from what is now known as the scheduled castes—an 'untouchable.'

Pappu Nayar accepted Bhargavi as his wife. He was blind from birth. Her reputation in the village was not good. No one questioned the propriety of his visiting that house of ill-repute. Was he not a blind man? Bhargavi's mother was fond of hearing stories from religious mythology and Pappu Nayar would narrate all the stories he knew. His mother had twice forbidden him to go there. Finally, Bhargavi became pregnant and Pappu Nayar acknowledged responsibility for this. His mother told him he would not be allowed to set foot in her house again. He replied, 'My younger brother isn't going to lead me around for ever. I need someone to look after me.' His expulsion from home became permanent.

Bhargavi worked as a sweeper in a *Brahmin* household. She was given two meals a day and five measures of rice every month.

Besides this, she was permanently engaged by two families to pound rice by hand. She looked after Pappu Nayar well. She would make *kanji* and feed him the rice while she had the water. She was an obedient girl and hardly ever talked. Misery appeared to have wiped out all traces of cheerfulness from her face. At twenty, her sunken eyes and cheeks and falling hair made her look ten years older. She never laughed out of a sense of inborn happiness. Occasionally, a derisive smile would play on her dried-up lips when she looked at her more fortunate companions.

Nearly always she managed with a thin loin cloth tied round her waist. She had hardly any other clothes to change into but she never hid her semi-nudity in shame.

Into that lifeless and drab atmosphere Pappu Nayar came with his light-hearted talk. He would say, 'Bhargavi has a boy in her womb. He'll grow up and recite the *Ramayana*.' She would reply, 'I want a girl.' She gave birth to a boy. Nayar's happiness was unbounded. He would not stir out of the room, telling all the women who called there, 'It's as I wanted. She wanted a girl'. He wanted to fondle the baby all the time. He would ask it, 'Well, little fellow, will you read the *Ramayana* to your father when you grow up?'

He would frequently ask her, 'Bhargavi, don't you ever kiss the baby?'

She would reply, 'Your tongue isn't idle even for a minute.'

'Woman, our good days have come. What more do I want? He'll take me to Kasi* and Rameswaram.* Won't you son?' Then he stroked the child and kissed it.

He began calculating the boy's horoscope. 'He's under the influence of Venus right from his youth. He's lucky. Bhargavi, we must name him Gopika Ramanan.' But she named him Raman. When he wanted to know why, she said, 'Oh, for a boy born to beg!'

'Don't say that, woman. His horoscope is that of a leader.'

The child would wriggle about on Pappu's lap and cry loudly. He would get excited and shout for Bhargavi. She would gnash her teeth and shout, 'The brat was born to scream.' She would beat the child and Pappu Nayar would be stunned. She went to work and returned only in the evening. He got anxious and started muttering to himself that the boy's throat was getting parched.

His affection was heart-rending. 'My son has great good fortune in store. Below his left breast there is a mole like a *lotus*—a sign of divine grace.' He would ask the women who lived nearby, 'Does he look like me?' Their eyes were wet with unshed tears. 'Can you see?' one asked.

'I can see my son,' he replied.

The women of the village said, 'Well she's a bad one all right. Does that child look like him?'

It was time for Raman to be given the first ceremonial morsel of rice. Pappu Nayar wanted to perform the auspicious act with his own hands but Bhargavi would not allow it. She told her mother that he had too big an appetite. Her mother said, 'Then we must get it done by someone else. He shouldn't grow up with a big appetite and a large tummy.'

'I didn't know I ate so much rice,' Pappu Nayar said, and laughed in genuine amusement.

The child grew up. Things started getting worse for the family. Bhargavi lost her job with the Brahmin household after being accused of theft.

'Don't keep the child hungry. Give him my share,' Pappu Nayar told her.

Then came the traditional time of scarcity. It was three days since even rice gruel had been cooked in the house. They managed on bean leaves, then on rice bran. On the third day, their neighbour, Kesavan Nayar, gave them a few pennies with which they bought a little rice to make into gruel. Bhargavi, her mother and the boy ate it. Pappu Nayar was sitting in the verandah, having the *Ramayana* read to him by a neighbour. He was not aware of what was going on.

That night he was singing couplets in praise of God. His gnawing hunger would not let him sleep even after midnight. The neighbours could hear him reciting the verses and beating time. Bhargavi became angry. 'What madness is this?'

'Wasn't I singing God's praises?' He stopped and prayed silently.

Bhargavi became pregnant again. He told her that this time she would have a girl. The boy had begun to talk a little. He would make the sounds for mother and grandmother but the sounds for 'father' never came from him. 'Little fellow,' Pappu Nayar would call out, 'Why don't you call out "father"?' And then he would console himself with the thought that the word for father was too difficult to pronounce.

Bhargavi gave birth to a girl. As before, he cast the child's horoscope and said that she was destined for a happy marriage in her fourteenth year.

'My daughter looks like her mother, doesn't she, sister?' he asked Kuttiyamma from next door. She laughed. 'Yes, I think so,' she replied.

Now there were two children. The family's poverty increased. Bhargavi's health was ruined and she was too weak to go to work. Pappu Nayar consoled her and told her that their poverty would soon end. She wanted to escape from all that misery by committing suicide. He argued that the children would be left motherless. Not a tear dropped from her eyes. She would just grind her teeth in helpless misery. Her lustreless, sunken eyes sometimes lit up for a moment with inhuman brightness but then she relapsed into a helpless acquiescence. One day she asked him, 'Why don't you go out and beg?'

'Woman, you're quite right. You're talking sense. But I'll have to leave the village. The problem is how can I go away from the little ones?'

Again Bhargavi became pregnant. This time she was too ill to get up. For many days there was not even a fire in the kitchen. Pappu Nayar would send Raman to the Brahmin houses at noon and the children and their mother would eat the *kanji* they got. Pappu Nayar would have some if anything was left over. He used to say, 'When I hear the *Ramayana* I want neither food nor drink.'

The children were left uncared-for. The boy was not to be seen during the day. He went from house to house begging. The girl fell ill. Pappu Nayar would borrow rice from some neighbour and get a bit of gruel prepared for her. When the boy came home at dusk and Pappu Nayar asked him to recite some words in praise of God, the boy would pay no heed. Nor would he sit and listen to Pappu

Nayar telling him stories of the gods and demons. Nayar knew he had gone only when he heard his voice from the kitchen.

The baby born to Bhargavi was a boy. It died on the fourth day which was a blessing. Pappu Nayar told Bhargavi, 'We have two children now; don't let's have any more.'

Raman was six years old and Pappu Nayar decided that he should go to school and be taught how to read and write. Bhargavi got back the job she had lost and the family could eat one meal a day. But Nayar continued to starve. Every day the mother and children would eat the food brought from the Brahmin house but Nayar was given something occasionally. He never asked for food and took what was given.

Raman stopped going to school. Bhargavi had decided she could not afford the expense and Pappu Nayar admitted she was right. All the same, his children should learn to read and write. But the boy was only six and they could wait for another year, Nayar said.

And the children? They never called him 'father' and would laugh when they saw him groping in his blind way.

'Daughter come here,' he would say and stretch out his hands. The girl would stand at a distance and make faces at him. Once he told Raman to bring him some *paan* and betel nuts. The boy spread the lime with a generous hand but put pebbles instead of arecanut.* Pappu Nayar got his mouth burnt. The boy clapped his hands and laughed. Nayar also laughed at the prank. One day he stepped down from the verandah to the front yard with the help of his stick. Raman threw the stick down and poor Nayar fell on his face. He described the events to passers-by as a boy's high spirits.

Two years went by and still Raman did not go to school. Whenever Pappu Nayar talked about this to Bhargavi, she would say, 'You can say anything you like with your glib tongue.' When he would ask her if there wasn't some truth in what he said, she would remain silent.

Raman was involved in some petty thieving. After all, he was a boy Nayar thought, consoling himself. Then, Bhargavi decided to send the boy to work as a domestic help. Nayar complained about it to Kuttiyamma. She had been an eye-witness to many of Bhargavi's goings-on. She had grieved over the way Pappu Nayar was ill-treated while Bhargavi ate her fill of rice and curry.

People began to talk but, out of sympathy for Nayar, nobody spoke directly to him and so the evil side of life lay hidden from him. People were afraid that he would not be able to bear the burden of the hell in which he lived if it was revealed to him. They admired his unbounded affection for Bhargavi and were amazed by his unshakable optimism. How could he be made to face stark reality?

Kuttiyamma could not bring herself to spell it out but when Pappu Nayar said, 'My son's a clever fellow. He'll learn to read and write,' she said, 'He is not your son.'

'No, he's a child of God. Isn't this world itself an illusion created by God?' She did not say anything to that. She did not have the strength to do so.

Bhargavi gave birth to a boy. Nayar was very happy at the new addition to the family. He said the child would be a companion for him. Kuttiyamma said, 'You're lucky you can't see. You don't have to see the misery and evil in this world.'

There's no evil in this world. True, there's poverty but that'll end. If there is sorrow, there is happiness also, sister. I'm not unhappy. God hasn't sent down any sorrows for me. Of course, I'm a little uneasy about my children. Raman hasn't even written me a letter.'

'You wouldn't feel like this if you'd seen those children.'

'I can see my children.'

'If so, are you their father?'

Kuttiyamma's heart missed a beat. She had blurted out the truth without thinking. Pappu Nayar hesitated, fumbling for an answer. 'They are children.'

'What do you know Pappu Nayar?'

'I'm not a fool, sister. Blind people have an excess of intelligence. I know many things. One night I heard the jingle of coins from inside the house.'

'She's evil!'

He did not answer immediately. 'What of it? At least the world won't say that the children have no father.'

'Do they call you father?'

'No, but I love them. Look, my Raman and Devaki are standing before me. How lovely they are! The little darlings!'

'She's been deceiving you.'

'She's to be pitied. How much she has endured! Perhaps this is her only way to survive. She requires a husband to show the world and I've been of help to her that way.'

Kuttiyamma left in silence. He was not someone groping in the dark. His mind was a luminous crystal with a perpetual inner-light. Many, many worlds flitted about playfully in that brilliant prism.

Further Reading

Thakazhi Pillai's major novels have been translated into English.
Two measures of Rice translated by M. A. Shakoor (Bombay), Jaico Publishing House, 1967.
Chemeen translated as 'The Shrimp' by Narayana Menon (London), Gollancz, 1968 (an award-winning novel about a girl from a fishing community who loves a boy from another religion).
The Iron Rod (New Delhi), Sterling Publishers, 1974.

For Malayali life, as seen by its writers, read *Malayalam Short Stories* (New Delhi), Sahitya Akademi, 1976.

Lajwanti

Rajinder Singh Bedi (1915–   )

Translated from the Urdu by Khushwant Singh. From *Contemporary Indian Short Stories,* selected and edited by Ka Naa Subramanyam (New Delhi) Vikas Publishing House, 1977

The Urdu short story which owes its modern form to Premchand enjoyed wide popularity in the 1940s when a group of writers with a special genius for this particular form of fiction came to the fore. This anthology has stories by three of them—Manto, Bedi and Qasmi. Bedi's plots are based on the commonplace rather than dramatic or melodramatic happenings and his portraits are of ordinary people like Lajwanti, the heroine of this story, and Rano, the central character of his award-winning novel *I Take This Woman.* Bedi does not idealise or sensationalise his heroines. Lajwanti's plea to be treated as an ordinary female and not a goddess on a pedestal echoes the author's philosophy.

Lajwanti is set against the background of Partition. The division between India and Pakistan caused riots between the two major religious communities and involved the displacement of millions of people. Women were raped and abducted. Societies were later set up to trace missing women and reunite them with their husbands or families. All too often, though, the victims found themselves rejected by their families who feared dishonour. In this classic story, the husband is an active social worker and a champion of reform yet he can only accept the return of his wife by regarding her as some sort of divine being and not as a woman.

'The leaves of the *lajwanti* wither with the touch of human hands.'

After the great holocaust, when people had washed the blood from their bodies, they turned their attention to those whose hearts had been torn by Partition. In every street and lane they set up a rehabilitation committee. In the beginning, people worked with great enthusiasm to rehabilitate refugees in work-camps, in homes and on the land. But there still remained the task of rehabilitating abducted women. Those that were recovered were brought back home but they ran into problems over this. The slogan of the supporters was 'Rehabilitate them in your hearts.' It was strongly opposed by the people living in the vicinity of the temple of Narain Bawa.

The campaign was started by the residents of Mulla Shakoor. They set up a Rehabilitation of Hearts Committee. A local lawyer was elected president. But the more important post of secretary went to Babu Sunder Lal who got a majority of eleven votes over his rival. It was the opinion of the old man who had written the petition and many other respectable citizens of the locality that no one would work more zealously than Sunder Lal because amongst the women abducted during the riots and not yet recovered, was Sunder Lal's wife, Lajwanti.

The Rehabilitation of Hearts Committee took out a daily procession through the streets at dawn. Whenever his friends, Rasalu and Neki Ram started singing the Punjabi folk song, 'The leaves of the lajwanti wither with the touch of human hands' as they went along, Sunder Lal would become silent. He would walk as if in a daze. Where in the name of God was Lajwanti? Was she thinking of him? Would she ever come back? . . . and his steps would falter on the smooth surface of the paved road.

Sunder Lal had abandoned all hope of finding Lajwanti. He had made his loss a part of the general loss. He had drowned his personal sorrow by plunging into social service. Even so, whenever he raised his voice to join the chorus, he could not help thinking, 'How fragile is the human heart . . . exactly like the lajwanti. One has only to bring a finger close to it and its leaves curl up.'

He had behaved very badly towards Lajwanti; he had allowed himself to be irritated with everything she did—even with the way she stood up or sat down, the way she cooked and the way she served his food; he had thrashed her many times. His poor Lajo,* who was as slender as the cypress tree! Life in the open air and sunshine had tanned her skin and filled her with an animal vitality. She ran about the lanes in their village with the mercurial grace of dew drops on a leaf. Her slim figure was full of robust health. When he first saw her, he was a little dismayed. Lajwanti took adversity in her stride including the chastisement he inflicted on her, so he increased the dose. But he was unaware of the limits of human endurance and Lajwanti's reactions were of little help. Even after the most violent thrashing she would break into giggles. 'If you beat me again, I'll never speak to you.'

Lajo forgot all about the beating as soon as it was over; all men beat their wives. If they did not, and let the women have their own way, the wives would be the first to say, 'What kind of man is he? He can't even manage a chit of girl like her!' They made up songs about the beatings men gave their women. Lajo had made a couplet which went something like this:— 'I will not marry a city lad as city lads wear boots and I have such a small bottom.'

Nevertheless, the first time Lajwanti met a boy from the city she fell in love with him. Sunder Lal had come with the bridegroom's party to Lajwanti's sister's wedding. He had seen Lajo and whispered in the bridegroom's ear, 'Your sister-in-law's quite a juicy morsel; your bride's likely to be a dainty dish, old chap!' Lajo had overheard him and the words went to her head. She did not notice the enormous boots Sunder Lal was wearing; she also forgot that her behind was small.

Such were the thoughts that coursed through his mind when he went out singing in the dawn procession. He would say to himself, 'If I were to get another chance, just one more chance, I'd really rehabilitate her in my heart. I would set an example to the people. These poor women are blameless; they were victimised by their lecherous ravishers. A society which refuses to accept these helpless women is rotten to the core and deserves to be destroyed.' He agitated for the rehabilitation of abducted women and for according them the respect due to a wife, mother, daughter and sister in the family. He exhorted the men never to remind these women of their past ordeals because they had become as sensitive as the lajwanti plant and would wither if a finger were pointed at them.

In order to propagate the cause of their society, the Mulla Shakoor Committee organised morning processions. The early hours of the dawn were blissfully peaceful—no hubbub or noise. Even the street dogs who had kept nocturnal vigils, were sound asleep beside the *tandoors*. People who were roused from their slumber by the singing would simply mutter, 'dawn chorus' and go back to their dreams.

People listened to Babu Sunder Lal's exhortations sometimes with patience, sometimes with irritation. Women who did not have any trouble in coming across from Pakistan were utterly complacent, like over-ripe cauliflowers while their men-folk were indifferent or grumbled and their children treated the songs of rehabilitation like lullabies to make them sleep.

Words which assail the ears in the early hours of the morning have a habit of going round one's head with insidious intent. Often a person who has not understood their meaning will find himself humming the phrases while he is going about his business. When Miss Mridula Sarabhai★ arranged for an exchange of abducted women between India and Pakistan, some of the male residents of Mulla Shakoor expressed their readiness to take them back. Their relatives went to receive them in the market place. For some time the abducted women and their menfolk faced each other in awkward silence. Then they swallowed their·pride, took their women and rebuilt their domestic lives. Rasalu, Neki Ram and Sunder Lal joined the throng and encouraged their supporters with slogans and the others joined in with 'Long live Mahinder Singh! Long live Sunder Lal!'

There were some who refused to have anything to do with the abducted women who were returned. 'Why couldn't they have killed themselves? Why didn't they take poison and preserve their virtue and their honour? Why didn't they jump into a well? They are cowards who clung to life . . .'

Hundreds of thousands of women had, in fact, killed themselves rather than be dishonoured. How could the dead know what courage it took to face the cold hostile world of the living, a hard-hearted world in which husbands refused to acknowledge their wives? And some of these women would think sadly of their names and the joyful meanings they had—Suhagwanti, or marital bliss—or they would turn to a younger brother and cry out, 'Oh Bihari, my own darling little brother, when you were a baby I looked after you as if you were my own son.' And Bihari would want to slip away into a corner but his feet would remain rooted to the ground and he would stare helplessly at his parents. The parents steeled their hearts and looked fearfully at their religious mentor, Narain Bawa, and Narain Bawa looked equally helplessly at heaven—the heaven that had no substance but is merely an optical illusion, a boundary beyond which we cannot see.

Miss Sarabhai brought a truck-load of Hindu women from Pakistan to be exchanged for Muslim women abducted by Indians. Lajwanti was not among them. Sunder Lal watched with hope and expectancy till the last of the Hindu women had come down from the truck. And then with patient resignation he plunged himself into the committee's activities again. The committee began to work twice as hard and more processions and meetings were organised. The aged lawyer, Kalka Prasad, addressed the meeting in his wheezy, asthmatic voice. Rasalu kept a spittoon in readiness beside him and strange noises came from the microphone when Kalka Prasad spoke.

Neki Ram also said a few words but whatever he said or quoted from the scriptures seemed to go against his point of view. Whenever the tide of battle appeared to be going against them, Babu Sunder Lal would rise and stem the retreat. He was never able to complete more than two sentences. His throat went dry and tears streamed down his face. His heart was always too full for words and he had to sit down, without making his speech. An embarrassed silence would descend on the audience. But the two sentences that Sunder Lal did utter came from the depths of his anguished heart and had a greater impact than all the clever arguments of the lawyer, Kalka Prasad. The men shed a few tears and lightened the burden pressing on their hearts; and then they went home without a thought in their empty heads.

One day, the Rehabilitation of Hearts Committee was out early in the afternoon. It trespassed into an arena near the temple which was looked upon as the citadel of orthodox reaction. The faithful were seated on a cement platform under the peepal tree listening to a commentary on the *Ramayana*. By sheer coincidence, Narain Bawa happened to be narrating the story about Rama* who, overhearing a washerman say to his errant wife, 'I am not Sri Ram Chandra* prepared to take back a woman who spent many years

83

with another man,' and was overcome by the implied rebuke and ordered his own wife, Sita, far gone with child, to leave his palace. 'Can one find a better example of the high standard of morality of that age?' asked Narain Bawa of his audience. 'Such was the sense of equality in the kingdom of Rama that even a poor washerman's remark was given full consideration. This was true Ram Rajya,* the Kingdom of God on earth.'

The procession had halted near the temple and had stopped to listen to the discourse. Sunder Lal heard the last sentence and spoke up. 'We don't want a Ram Rajya of this sort.'

'Be quiet! Who's this man? Silence!' came the cries from the audience.

Sunder Lal forced his way through the crowd and said loudly, 'No one can stop me from speaking. . . .'

Another volley of protest came from the devout. 'Silence! We'll not let you say a single word!' And someone shouted from a corner, 'We'll kill you!'

Narain Bawa spoke gently, 'My dear Sunder Lal, you do not understand the sacred traditions of the *Vedas*.'

Sunder Lal was ready with his retort, 'I understand at least one thing: in Ram Rajya the voice of a washerman was heard but the present-day champions of that same Ram Rajya cannot bear to hear the voice of Sunder Lal.'

The people who had threatened to beat him up were put to shame. 'Let him speak,' and 'Silence, let's hear him,' were heard from many and Sunder Lal began. 'Sri Rama was our hero but what kind of justice did he practise when he accepted the word of a washerman but refused to believe his own wife!' Turning to Narain Bawa he said, 'Bawaji, there are many things in the world which are beyond my comprehension. I believe that the only true Ram Rajya is a state where a person neither does wrong to anyone nor suffers anyone to do him wrong.'

Sunder Lal's words attracted everybody's attention. 'Injustice to oneself,' he went on, 'is as great a wrong as inflicting it on others. Lord Rama evicted Sita from his home only because she was compelled to live with her abductor, Ravana. What sin did Sita ever commit? Wasn't she the victim of a ruse and then of violence like our own mothers and sisters today? Was it a question of Sita's morality or the wickedness of Ravana? Today our innocent Sitas have been thrown out of their own homes. Sita . . . Lajwanti . . .' Sunder Lal broke down and wept.

Rasalu and Neki Ram raised their banners high; school children had cut out and pasted slogans on them. They yelled, 'Long live Sunder Lal!' and somebody in the crowd shouted, 'Long live Sita, the queen of virtue!' Somebody else cried out for Sri Rama Chandra but many called out 'Silence!' They left the congregation to join the procession, and Narain Bawa's months of preaching were undone in a few moments. They sang as they marched to the great square, 'The leaves of the lajwanti wither at the touch . . .'

The dawn had not yet turned grey in the eastern horizon when the procession's songs began to wake up the residents of Mulla Shakoor. The widow in house 414 stretched her limbs and went back to her dreams; but Lal Chand who was from Sunder Lal's village came running. He stuck his arms out of his shawl and said panting, 'Congratulations Sunder Lal. I've seen Lajo *Bhabi.*'

Sunder Lal, who had been prodding the embers in the clay bowl of his hookah, let it fall from his hands and the sweetened tobacco scattered on the floor. 'Where did you see her?' he asked.

'On the border at Wagah.

'It must have been someone else,' he said and quickly sat down on his haunches.

'No brother Sunder Lal, it was Lajo Bhabi,' repeated Lal Chand with assurance. 'The same Lajo.'

'Could you recognise her?' asked Sunder Lal, gathering bits of tobacco and smashing them in his palm. 'All right, tell me what are her distinguishing marks?'

'You're a strange one to suppose I wouldn't recognise her! She has a tattoo mark on her chin, another one on her right cheek and . . .'

'Yes, yes,' exploded Sunder Lal and completed his wife's description. 'The third one is on her forehead.'

He sat up on his knees. He wanted to remove all doubt. He recalled all the marks that had been tattooed on her body as a child. They were the green spots on the leaves of the lajwanti which disappear when the leaves curl up. His Lajwanti had behaved in exactly the same way: whenever he pointed out her tattoo marks she used to curl up in embarrassment—almost as if she were being stripped and her nakedness was being exposed. A strange longing as well as fear wracked his body. He took Lal Chand by the arm and asked, 'How did Lajo get to the border?'

'There was an exchange of abducted women between India and Pakistan.'

'So what happened?' Sunder Lal stood up suddenly and repeated with impatience, 'Tell me what happened then.'

Rasalu rose from the *charpoy*. 'Is it really true that Lajo Bhabi's back?'

Lal Chand went on with his story. 'At the border, the Pakistanis returned sixteen of our women and took back sixteen of theirs. There was some argument and our men said that the women they were handing over were old or middle-aged and of little use. A large crowd gathered and hot words were exchanged. Then one of their fellows got Lajo to stand up on the top of the truck, snatched her *dupatta* off and asked them if she could be described as an old woman. "Take a good look at her," they said. "Can one amongst those you're returning measure up to her?" And Lajo Bhabi was overcome with embarrassment and tried to hide her tattoo marks. The argument became very heated and both parties threatened to take back their goods. I cried out to her in the tumult but our police cracked down on us.' He bared his elbow to show the mark of a *lathi* blow. Rasalu and Neki Ram remained silent. Sunder Lal stared vacantly into space.

He was getting ready to go to the border at Wagah when he heard of Lajo's return. He became nervous and could not make up his mind whether to go to meet her or wait for her at home. He wanted to run away, to spread out all the banners and placards he had carried and cry to his heart's content. But, like other men, all he did was to go to the police station as if nothing untoward had happened. And suddenly he found his Lajo standing in front of him. She looked scared and trembled like a peepal leaf in the breeze. He looked up. His Lajwanti had wrapped her dupatta round her head like a Muslim woman. He was also upset by the fact that she looked healthier than before. Her complexion was clearer and she had put on weight. He had sworn to say nothing to his wife but he could not understand why, if she was happy, she had come back. Had the government forced her to return against her will?

There were many men at the police station. Some were refusing to take back their women. 'We won't take these sluts, left over by the Muslims,' they said. Sunder Lal overcame his revulsion. He had thrown himself, body and soul, into this movement and there were his colleagues yelling slogans in raucous voices over the microphone. Through the babble of speeches and slogans Sunder Lal and Lajo proceeded to their home. The scene of a thousand years ago was being repeated: Sri Ram Chandra and Sita returning to Ayodhya after their long exile. Some people had lit lamps of joy to welcome them while at the same time washing away the sins which had forced an innocent couple to suffer such hardship.

Sunder Lal continued to work with the Rehabilitation of Hearts Committee with the same zeal. He fulfilled the pledge he had taken in spirit and even those who had suspected him to be an armchair reformer were converted. But there were others who could not accept Lajwanti and the widow in number 414 was not the only one who stayed away from Sunder Lal's house. He had nothing but contempt for these people. The queen of his heart had returned and his once silent temple now resounded with laughter. He had installed a living idol in his innermost sanctum and sat outside the gate like a sentry. Sunder Lal no longer called Lajwanti by her name; he addressed her as a goddess—Devi.★ She responded to his affection and began to open up, as her namesake unfurls its leaves. She was deliriously happy and wanted to tell her husband all her experiences and by her tears wash away her sins. But Sunder Lal would not let her broach the subject. At night she would stare at his face and when he asked her why she could offer no explanation. And the tired Sunder Lal would fall asleep.

Only on the first day after her return had he asked her about her 'black days.' Who was he? Lajwanti had lowered her eyes and replied,' *Jumma.*' Then she looked at him directly as if she wanted to ask him something but Sunder Lal had a queer look in his eyes and started playing with her hair. She dropped her eyes. He asked, 'Was he good to you?'

'Yes.'

'Didn't he beat you then?'

Lajwanti leaned back and rested her head on Sunder Lal's chest. 'No, he never said a thing to me. He didn't beat me but I was terrified of him. You used to beat me but I was never afraid of you. You won't beat me again, will you?'

Sunder Lal's eyes filled with tears. In a voice full of remorse and shame he said, 'No, Devi, never. I shall never beat you again.'

'Goddess.' Lajo pondered over the word for a while and then began to sob. She wanted to tell him everything but Sunder Lal stopped her. 'Let's forget the past. You didn't commit any sin. It is the social system that refuses to give an honoured place to virtuous women like you, that's evil.'

Lajwanti's secret remained locked in her breast. She looked at her own body which had since Partition become the body of a goddess. It no longer belonged to her. She was blissfully happy but her happiness was tinged with a superstitious fear that it would not last. Many days passed in this way. Suspicion took the place of joy not because Sunder Lal had begun to ill-treat her but because he treated her too well. She had never expected him to be so considerate and wanted him to be the old Sunder Lal with whom she used to quarrel over a carrot and who would try to make amends with a radish. Now there were no quarrels. Sunder Lal made her feel like fragile glass that would break at the slightest touch. She took to gazing at herself in the mirror. In the end she could no longer recognise herself. She had been rehabilitated but not accepted. Sunder Lal refused to see her tears or to hear her wailing. Every morning he went out with the procession. Lajwanti, dragging her tired body to the window, would hear the song whose words no one understood, 'The leaves of the lajwanti wither at the touch of human hands . . .'

Further Reading

Bedi's short stories have yet to be translated but his award-winning novel, *I Take This Woman,* is available in English translation by Khushwant Singh (New Delhi), Orient Paperbacks, 1967. It is the story of a Punjab village woman whose community custom forces her to marry her young brother-in-law when her own husband is murdered.

Stench of Kerosene

Amrita Pritam (1919–   )

Translated from the Punjabi by Khushwant Singh. From *Land of Five Rivers: Stories from the Punjab,* edited by Khushwant Singh and Jaya Thadani (Bombay), Jaico Publishing House, 1965

Amrita Pritam is regarded as one of the foremost poets of the subcontinent. Her use of a ballad-like poetic form for her famous elegy on the country's partition, and subsequent poems in which she used traditional Punjabi folk heroes, launched her as one of the major creative and passionate talents since independence. Since then she has experimented with free verse and her latest work is highly sophisticated. In her fiction she is essentially a writer about love in all its aspects and her subjects range from upper-class educated and liberated women to the heroine of this tragic village tale. Though the setting is localised to a village in the Kulu valley, the rejection of a childless woman is widespread in the subcontinent and many other parts of the world.

Outside, a mare neighed. Guleri recognised the neighing and ran out of the house. The mare was from her parents' village. She put her head against its neck as if it were the door to her father's house.

Guleri's parents lived in Chamba. A few miles from her husband's village which was on high ground, the road curved and descended steeply downhill. From this point one could see Chamba lying a long way away at one's feet. Whenever Guleri was homesick she would take her husband, Manak, and go up to this point. She would see the homes of Chamba twinkling in the sunlight and would come back, her heart glowing with pride.

Once every year, after the harvest had been gathered in, Guleri was allowed to spend a few days with her parents. They sent a man to Lakarmandi to bring her back to Chamba. Two of her friends, who were also married to boys who lived away from Chamba, came home at the same time and the girls looked forward to their annual reunion, talking about their joys and sorrow. They went about the streets together. Then there was the harvest festival when the girls would have new clothes made for the occasion. Their *dupattas* would be dyed, starched and sprinkled with mica to make them glisten. They would buy glass bangles and silver ear-rings.

Guleri always counted the days to the harvest. When autumn breezes cleared the skies of monsoon clouds, she thought of little else. She went about her daily chores—fed the cattle, cooked food for her parents-in-law—and then sat back to work out how long it would be before someone came to fetch her from her parent's village.

And now, once again, it was time for her annual visit. She caressed the mare joyfully, greeted her father's servant, Natu, and made preparations to leave the next day. She did not have to express her excitement in words: the look on her face was enough. Her husband pulled at his *hookah* and closed his eyes. It seemed as if he either did not like the tobacco or that he could not bear to face his wife.

'You'll come to the fair at Chamba, won't you? Come even for a day,' she pleaded.

Manak put aside his *chillum* but did not reply. 'Why don't you answer me?' she asked, a little cross. 'Shall I tell you something?'

'I know what you're going to say—that you only go to your parents once a year. Well you've never been stopped before.'

'Then why do you want to stop me this time?' she demanded.

'Just this once,' he pleaded.

'Your mother's said nothing so why do you stand in the way?' Guleri was childishly stubborn.

'My mother . . .' Manak did not finish his sentence.

On the long-awaited morning, Guleri was ready long before dawn. She had no children and therefore no problem of having to leave them behind or take them with her. Natu saddled the mare as she took leave of Manak's parents. They patted her head and blessed her.

'I'll come with you for part of the way,' Manak said.

Guleri was happy as they set out. She hid Manak's flute under her *dupatta*.

After the village of Khajiar, the road descended steeply to Chamba. There she took out the flute and gave it to him. She took his hand in hers and said, 'Come now, play your flute.' But Manak, lost in his thoughts, paid no heed. 'Why don't you play your flute?' she asked, coaxing him. He looked at her sadly. Then putting the flute to his lips, blew a strange anguished wail.

'Guleri, don't go away,' he begged her. 'I ask again, don't go away this time.' He handed the flute to her, unable to continue.

'But why?' she asked. 'Come over on the day of the fair and we'll return together, I promise you.'

Manak did not ask again.

They stopped by the roadside. Natu took the mare a few paces ahead to leave the couple alone. It crossed Manak's mind that it was at this time of the year, seven years ago, that he and his friends had come on this very road to go to the harvest festival in Chamba. And it was at this fair that Manak had first seen Guleri and they had bartered their hearts to each other. Later, managing to meet her alone, he remembered taking her hand and telling her, 'You are like unripe corn—full of milk.'

'Cattle go for unripe corn,' Guleri had replied, freeing her hand with a jerk. 'Human beings prefer it roasted. If you want me, go and ask my father for my hand.'

Among Manak's kinsmen it was customary to settle the bride price* before the wedding. Manak was nervous because he did not know the price Guleri's father would demand from him. But Guleri's father was prosperous and had lived in cities. He had sworn that he would not take money for his daughter but would give her to a worthy young man from a good family. Manak, he decided, answered these requirements and soon after, Guleri and Manak were married. Deep in memories, Manak was roused by Guleri's hand on his shoulder.

'What are you dreaming of?' she teased him.

He did not answer. The mare neighed impatiently and Guleri got up to leave. 'Do you know the bluebell wood a couple of miles from here?' she asked. 'It's said that anyone who goes through it becomes deaf. You must have passed through that bluebell wood. You don't seem to be hearing anything I say.'

'You're right, Guleri. I can't hear anything you're saying to me,' and Manak sighed.

They looked at each other. Neither understood the other's thoughts. 'I'll go now,' Guleri said gently. 'You'd better go back. You've come a long way from home.'

'Youv'e walked all the distance. You'd better get on the mare,' replied Manak.

'Here, take your flute.'

'You take it.'

'Will you come and play it on the day of the fair?' she asked with a smile. The sun shone in her eyes. Manak turned his face away. Perplexed, Guleri shrugged her shoulders and took the road to Chamba. Manak returned home.

He entered the house and slumped listlessly on the *charpoy*. 'You've been away a long time,' exclaimed his mother. 'Did you go all the way to Chamba?'

Not all the way, only to the top of the hill.' Manak's voice was heavy.

'Why do you croak like an old woman?' said his mother severely. 'Be a man.'

Manak wanted to retort, 'You are a woman; why don't you cry like one for a change!' But he remained silent.

Manak and Guleri had been married seven years but she had never borne a child and Manak's mother had made a secret resolve that she would not let it go beyond the eighth year. This year, true to her decision, she had paid five hundred *rupees* to get him a second wife and she was waiting, as Manak knew, for Guleri to go to her parents before bringing in the new bride. Obedient to his mother and to custom, Manak's body responded to the new woman but his heart was dead within him.

In the early hours one morning he was smoking his chillum when an old friend happened to pass by. 'Ho, Bhavani, where are you going so early in the morning?'

Bhavani stopped. He had a small bundle on his shoulder.' Nowhere in particular,' he said evasively.

'You should be on your way to some place or the other,' exclaimed Manak. 'What about a smoke?'

Bhavani sat down on his haunches and took the chillum from Manak's hands. 'I'm going to Chamba for the fair,' he said at last.

Bhavani's words pierced through Manak's heart like a needle.

'Is the fair today?'

'It's the same day, every year,' replied Bhavani drily. 'Don't you remember, we were in the same party seven years ago?' Bhavani did not say any more but Manak was conscious of the other man's rebuke and he felt uneasy. Bhavani put down the chillum and picked up his bundle. His flute was sticking out of the bundle. Manak's eye remained on the flute till Bhavani disappeared from view.

Next morning, Manak was in his fields when he saw Bhavani coming back but he looked the other way deliberately. He did not want to talk to Bhavani to hear anything about the fair. But Bhavani came round the other side and sat down in front of Manak. His face was sad and grey as a cinder.

'Guleri is dead,' Bhavani said in a flat voice.

'What?'

'When she heard of your second marriage, she soaked her clothes in kerosene and set fire to them.'

Manak, mute with pain, could only stare and feel his own life burning out.

The days went by. Manak resumed his work in the fields and ate his meals when they were given to him. But he was like a dead man, his face blank, his eyes empty.

'I am not his wife,' complained his second wife. 'I'm just someone he happened to marry.'

But quite soon she was pregnant and Manak's mother was pleased with her new daughter-in-law. She told Manak about his wife's condition, but he looked as if he did not understand and his eyes were still empty.

His mother encouraged her daughter-in-law to bear with her husband's moods for a few days. As soon as the child was born and placed in his father's lap, she said, Manak would change.

A son was duly born to Manak's wife; and his mother, rejoicing, bathed the boy, dressed him in fine clothes and put him in Manak's lap. Manak stared at the new-born babe in his lap. He stared a long time, uncomprehending, his face as usual expressionless. Then suddenly the blank eyes filled with horror and Manak began to scream. 'Take him away!' he shrieked hysterically, 'Take him away! He stinks of kerosene.'

Further Reading

A great many of Amrita Pritam's prose works and some of her poetry have been translated into English.

Skeleton (New Delhi) Orient Paperback, 1973 (one of her best known novellas; it deals with the theme of abduction).

A Line in Water (New Delhi), Arnold/Heinemann, 1975 (a study of 'upper crust' Punjabi society).

Compulsions

Ahmad Nadim Qasmi (1920–   )

Translated from the Urdu by Ralph Russell. From *Ghar se Ghar Tak* (Rawalpindi) Kitab Ghar, 1965.

Like so many of his peers, Qasmi made his name both as a poet and as a short-story writer in the 1940's. He writes about his native Punjab villages and villagers. Many of his stories deal with the changes in attitudes towards marriage and, of course, as in *Compulsions,* the many compromises in religious beliefs and customs demanded by so-called 'Westernisation'.

It was a strange thing that here was Amin, an accountant with David and David Ltd, wearing coat and trousers, and speaking half-English Urdu, when he spoke it at all; and there in the village his fianceé was still scaring birds from the fields and singing the *mahia.* Amin had become so used to town life that when he took leave and visited the village, he used to bring home lots of loaves of English-style bread so that he should not be deprived of his buttered toast for breakfast. While his mother made the toast on the iron plate, he would think to himself that Banu would be churning the curd at that very moment; and while his mother was putting sugar in his tea, Banu would be stirring salt into the bowl of *lassi,* with her ear-rings, hidden beneath her small plaits, clashing together, and the shadow of her long dense eyelashes falling on her cheeks and the blue veins showing up on her neck which was white as butter.

It was strange, too, that whenever Amin thought about the social gap between Banu and himself, his thoughts would turn in the end to Banu's neck and to her neckline. That was why, in spite of his own purely urban life-style, he maintained his engagement to this awkward village girl. In the quarter of the city where he lived and in the office where he worked, he had been offered many a good match, but the excellence of the match had centred not on the girl's beauty but on her dowry or on her parent's wealth. Granted that from an aesthetic point of view wealth is nothing very beautiful, from an economic point of view it has considerable charm; but Amin's subconscious was still rooted in the village. With the first drops of rain, when the whole air was fragrant with the sweet smell of the earth, he would feel an impulse to go out and embrace the wet soil. He liked the rose because it *was* a rose, not because it was the raw material of rose candy. And this was why, when a match was proposed to him, he would first turn his attention to the girl and not to the silver and gold that went with her; and whenever he did this, the picture of Banu churning the curd and faintly smiling would rise before him. Then, instead of talking about the proposed match, he would start talking about the weather.

When the news reached his village that Amin had become an accountant in a British firm at 350 rupees a month, Banu's parents at once stopped her going to the well for water; and Banu wept so much at this prohibition that you would have thought that she had been suddenly put into solitary confinement. That day she re-membered vividly everything that lay on the path from her house to the well, things which she had never even thought of looking at before—the purple flower on the bush by the blacksmith's house; *Mir,* Dad's dog which sat all day at the door of his house, staring brazenly at the girls going to and fro; the creeper climbing all over the tree in Sher Khan's courtyard and hanging down into the lane—the creeper, which, when the children gave a little tug at its yellow trailers, would make the tree shake right up to the top; the messenger who came from the nearby town, whose moustache turned upwards on one side while the other side turned down; the dirty jokes that Nuran, the barber's wife, told at the well. The girls would listen to them, put their hands to the lobes of their ears, and cry *'Tauba! Tauba!'* and then would laugh heartily. Banu felt as though the whole village had suddenly been taken from her, and when her father left the house, she complained to her mother, 'Mum, do what you like with me but don't make me a lady!' Her mother laughed at this just as a mother-in-law laughs when her daughter-in-law feels the first pains and cries out 'Oh God, I don't want to have a child!'

When Amin came to the village to make arrangements for the wedding and his mother told him happily, 'Banu no longer goes to the well to draw water,' he didn't like it at all. 'Why not?' he said. 'Why doesn't she go? I'm not marrying Banu because her father is Dad's best friend or because her people have enough wheat to last them right through to the next harvest. I'm marrying her because she's a simple village girl and . . .'

And . . .? But how could he tell his mother. Because when she comes along with two full pitchers of water on her head all the curves of her body stand out. Because when she takes food to her father in the fields at mid-day and there is nobody in sight then she begins softly humming the *mahia*. Because while her father is eating, she gets out her catapult and scares the birds off the millet crop with cries of 'Ha ha! Ha ha! Ho! Do Do!' Because she can lift great bundles of hay to put down for the cows to eat, and when the cows get the chance they lick her back and she scolds them as though she were scolding the girls she played with. Because she churns the curd, and turns her sleeves up to her shoulders and makes butter. Because she quarrels with the women who come to sell vegetables, waving her hands about and arguing over the price of every carrot. Because when her friends get married she dances the *luddi* with such vigour as to put the professional dancers to shame. How lovely she looks at such times! Of course, he could not say all that so he simply said, 'and . . . I don't like it at all.'

'*Why* don't you like it?' his mother asked him. 'You don't like the *parathas* I cook, so you bring these wretched puffy loaves with you from the city. And yet you like it when Banu roams all over the village wherever she likes. Why? But then you were just the same when you were a child. If I cooked *dal* you would cry your eyes out and then pick up an onion and start eating it.' His mother was laughing at him and all Amin could do was think to himself, 'All right, wait till I'm married and back in Lahore. *Then* we'll see whether anyone restricts her or not.'

Two days after the wedding, Banu's brother came to take her back to her mother's house. Banu pulled the border of her silk shawl well over her face, with her jewellery clinking and her gold-starred embroidery shining, and went off with her brother, her girl friends and the dancing women. Amin felt like running forward and pulling the border of her shawl so far forward that her lowered, attractive eyes, her thin and prominent nose, her well-formed upper lip and sharp-cornered mouth, and the fresh rose petals of her cheeks would be hidden completely from sight. He felt agitated, got up, and paced up and down for a long time as though the army of his honour and self-respect was being defeated on the battlefield of Waterloo.

When he came out of the lane, the breeze struck him, laden with the intoxicating perfume of henna. He felt as though all the people passing through the lane were dilating their nostrils and taking in deep breaths, taking in the perfume which Banu's palms and feet were spreading so generously. And then he had a sort of feeling that at the corner of the lane the few sparks which he could see flashing were the stars of Banu's embroidery; and he felt as though suddenly some young man had turned into the lane, turned back, snatched the embroidery and gone off with it; and Amin felt an impulse to chase after him, grab him, and twist his arm until he could wrest it from his hands.

When Banu's new *burqa* of fine rustling white cloth came from the tailor she sat there as though in dread all day. When her mother-in-law sang the praises of the fine network over the eyes and the little pleats of the headpiece, Banu felt like a goat set down before the butcher to listen to the praises of the sharp edge of his knife. She longed to weep and wail aloud and when, at last, night came and she was alone, she seized the opportunity, as though her stolen property had been returned to her and cried to her heart's content. When Amin came, took her face in both hands and went to kiss her, he saw that she was crying, crying so much that even the top of her blouse was wet; and when he found out why she was crying and sobbing like a child, he held up her head with his left hand and with his right wiped the tears from her cheeks and told her that times change. 'Once we used to travel on mules and camels. Now there are roads running through our villages and buses running on them. Is that anything to cry about? My forefathers in that same village used to do the ploughing themselves, but now they have tenants to do it. Would they cry over that? Today in our village in the big houses the women sit secluded in *purdah*. Their grandmothers, like you, used to cut the hay and scare off the birds from the crops. Do you think that when their families got rich and they were put into purdah they cried about it? Here in the village you used not to wear the burqa because when you're wearing a burqa you can't draw water from the well or work in the fields. But in the city you won't have to do these things and there, in all the houses where I live, the women observe purdah. And when we get to Lahore we'll make this white burqa into a pillow case and table cloths and I'll get a black silk burqa made for you, even if it costs me half my salary.'

On the day when Amin took his wife with him to the bus station to go to Lahore, he was fighting with himself. If the fine network was not quite adequate to conceal the lines of Banu's long black eyelashes, what of it? This same Banu who was stumbling in this awkward way as she went along in her burqa once used to leap like a young deer on these same paths. So if people could glimpse the arches of her eyebrows through the network of the burqa, what of it? But even as he felt this, he felt also a strange pain in his heart, as if everybody as the bus station was staring at the network on Banu's burqa. These days people are so experienced in these things that simply by looking at a woman's little finger they can form an idea of her features, and in Banu's case her eyes were almost entirely visible.

All the way to Lahore he kept looking at the other pasengers in the bus, suspecting all the time that they were looking at Banu. The smallest thing made him feel as though all the blood were rushing to his head. At one point, Banu took her hennaed hand out of her burqa and put it on the back of the seat in front of her. Amin's face reddened as though he thought that all the passengers in the bus were talking about his wife's hand. He told her to cover up her hand. She turned round quickly and looked at him, and them drew her hand back into her burqa so sharply that you would have thought that if she could have shaken it from her wrist she would have thrown it out of the moving bus.

After they reached Lahore Banu was at first uneasy within the four walls of Amin's little house; but then she settled down. Meanwhile, Amin was explaining to his close friends that the main thing in life is experience. 'Without experience, the only difference between a man and a donkey is that a man has two legs and a donkey has four. Experience alone makes a man a man, and then a civilised, cultured man. What do the Eskimoes know of the pleasure of the cool shade? I used to think that beauty was riches that ought to be spent, but now experience has shown me that the proper place for these riches is in the security bank of the home.' When they heard such words coming from their enlightened companion all of Amin's friends laughed, but it wasn't the laughter of ridicule. On the contrary, these clerks, head clerks and office superintendents felt that they had rescued an intelligent young man from falling prey to the curse of free thinking.

When Banu's black silk burqa came from the tailor's, it suddenly dawned upon her too that she was making progress. This dawning sense became a certainty when a few months later she went to her village to a relative's wedding. When she got down at the bus station with her silk burqa undulating like the waves of the sea, and her husband followed her in his tie and suit, and their leather suitcases were taken down from the roof of the bus, everyone stood there holding their breath as though a plane had landed at the bus station. When the village girls came, not so much to meet her as to see her—the same girls with whom she had sung the mahia and danced the luddi and plied the spinning wheel—she formed the firm conviction that she was a being separate from and superior to all of them. The fine red polish on her toenails gleamed like burning coals. Her moist dark-red lips were like a fresh wound. The line of *surma* along her eyelids was extended to her temples. In her hand she held a little handkerchief, and her colourful silk *shalwar* fitted her so closely that you could even see the circle of her navel. The other women threw small coins to the dansing girls when they sang, but Banu put her hand into the neck of her jumper and pulled out 4-anna and 8-anna pieces to throw at them; and when her former playmates asked her to tell them about Lahore she told more lies and bigger lies than she had ever told before in all her life. When she stood up and wrapped her burqa around her and then, throwing back the double veil over her head, put on her gold sandals and smilingly said goodbye, the women could smell for a long time the fragrance of the delicate perfume which her rustling burqa was shedding.

Now Banu's burqa, like her nail polish and her lipstick, became an essential part of her adornments. On the evening of the first day of each month she joined a party of her women neighbours to go shopping after which she would spend hours ironing her burqa. Amin had moved to another firm at double the pay he had been getting and so had rented part of a large house. He had also engaged a maid-servant for Banu, bought himself a scooter, and begun to wear a dressing gown. He got a three-piece suite and little glass-topped tables for his sitting room and every week to ten days had begun to invite his office friends home. His friends now came from a different class. A few of them had wives who no longer observed purdah and sometimes the wives, too, would come to his parties. They would go into the house for a little while to say hello to Banu, but most of the time they would stay with the men talking about everything from world politics to purdah, and the price of cabbages, and the adulteration of chillies. On occasion too, the higher officials of these firms and their wives would be present at these parties and all the wives would mix as though they had been childhood playmates. Then, one day, Amin learnt that one of his colleagues had suddenly been promoted and that the reason was that his wife had become friendly with the boss's wife—so friendly, in fact, that they even exchanged gifts or sweetmeats at Id.★

'That's not right,' Amin said to himself. 'That's sheer shameless-ness. That's as if I were to invite my boss to a party and tell my wife to put the food in his mouth with her own hands. No sir, we're not going to do that. We're village people really, and if we begin to think on these lines who knows where it will all end? No, my friend, we're not going to be so brazen.'

God knows how many clerks were using their wives as rungs on the ladder to promotion, climbing quickly, while Amin was taking years to achieve the advancement that others were achieving in months. Quite a few men who had come to the firm after him, as his juniors, now ranked above him. In spite of this, he seemed resigned and contented with his lot. Every year he got an increase in pay according to the rules of the firm and, in this way, after a few years he reached a position where he could leave his annexe and move into a little bungalow. He sold his scooter, bought a little car and began to shave twice a day.

In the meantime, Banu had borne him three children. The eldest boy had been sent to a convent school and was already saying, 'Good morning' and 'Ta, ta.' And Banu had begun to tell stories to her children in which the fairies ate English cake and built their palaces amidst the flowers of Hyde Park. They would fall in love with princes and pursue them, flying from London to Paris or Berlin, or, at the furthest, Istanbul. She would sing them songs like 'Cock-a-doodle-do.' As a matter of fact, Amin had started educating Banu as soon as they were married, beginning with the ABC. By the time they had moved to a bungalow, and started going for outings in the car, and having early morning tea just like English people, and exclaiming 'Good God!' when they were surprised or delighted, Banu could read the books of fairy stories fluently. She would no longer tell visitors that she was the daughter of a farmer, but would say, 'Daddy has always liked to live on his farm, like Eisenhower.'

In spite of all this, her purdah had become an article of faith with her. Even when she could hear hysterical laughter coming from the drawing room, she would lower her voice to talk to her children, her servants and her maids, as though all the world was straining its ears to listen to her. When there was a party Amin would sometimes come out of the dining room into the corridor and call out, 'Bania, darling, my cigarettes are on the shelf. Bring them to me please.' And afterwards Banu would scold him and tell him that when you call out to women who observe purdah you shouldn't call them by name. Amin would laugh and say, 'Yes, I know that; but I call you by name in case my friends think that I'm a widower.'

When Amin pulled up in front of the firm's office and got out of his car he looked at the cars of his superiors and felt as though he was getting out of a little tin box. And when he left his room to take some files to show to a superior, who at one time had to bring files to show *him,* he felt as though a pill of quinine was dissolving at the root of his tongue. And when he saw his superior's reflection in the glass surface of the great long table, as though he were peering into a lake rather than signing a paper, then his blood boiled and his temples began to ache. At night he did his best to be the last to leave the office because once when his car wouldn't start one of his friends had called out to him, 'Come on Amin, get into my car and put your car in the boot.' Even the orderlies had smiled.

The best that Amin could do to hide his sense of inferiority was to invite his superiors to his parties, feed them lavishly and laugh loudly at their empty jokes. He did not drink, but he would occasionally take a hint from one of his superiors and lay on drinks too. On occasion, when these superiors got a bit merry, he had had to listen to such remarks as 'Amin, aren't you ever going to introduce us to your wife? When's it to be?' And on one or two occasions his boss had got drunk, gone into the corridor and shouted '*Bhabhi!* Bhabhi dear!' and Amin had had to restrain him. His boss had replied, 'Oh *You* can see *my* wife but I can't see yours, is that it?' There had been bad feeling between them but the very next day when he got to the office the first thing he did was to go to his boss and apologise.

About this time, one of his juniors in the firm got married and threw a whole series of parties. His wife was a smooth young woman who had spent a year at college and could manage to speak a whole English sentence without once saying, 'You see.' Within a few months this man had been promoted over Amin. On the first occasion when this fellow, who had always called him 'Sir,' addressed him as Mr Amin, he was momentarily paralysed. Then he recovered himself and said, 'Sir, I'm having a small drinks party tomorrow night to celebrate your promotion; will you and your wife be able to join us?'

The following evening when his guests assembled and the glasses were set out on the table, Amin opened a large bottle of White Horse and began as usual to pour the drinks. His guest of honour said, 'Who is this glass for?'

'Me,' Amin replied.

They all held their breath. Only the women seemed a little taken aback. All of them shouted excitedly, 'No!'

'Why not?' said Amin; and he raised the glass like a practised drinker.

'Hurrah!' they all shouted.

Three rooms away, Banu stopped in the midst of giving instructions to her servants and her maids and for a long time looked with a frown towards the door that opened into the corridor, and then turned to scold the servants.

After a while, Banu began to feel as though she was sitting not in her house but in the fish market. The noise coming from the drawing room was loud and continuous. People were shouting at the top of their voices until they were practically screaming, and the laughter of the women cut like a knife. She felt panicky, and glanced towards the door of the children's room; but it was shut. She began to feel ashamed in the presence of the servant standing in front of her.

'Ask your master to come here,' she said to him.

He went off, came back and stood quietly in front of her.

'Did you ask him?' Banu said, looking at his shocked face.

'Yes, he's . . .' He blinked and began to wring his hands nervously.

A moment later it was Banu's turn to look shocked. She glanced towards the door leading into the corridor and at once turned back, afraid.

Led by Amin, his friends and their wives filed in together. The loose ends of the women's saris were slipping down from their shoulders and the bottom edge of their blouses had ridden up. They were laughing all the time. As soon as they came in they went and stood like sentries at the doors of the children's room and the bathroom. There was nowhere for Banu to run to. She pressed herself to the wall and hid her face in her stole.

They were all swaying as they tried to keep their balance, standing with their feet wide apart, and Amin was in such a state that you would have thought that he was doing gymnastics.

Amin was completely drunk; it seemed as though his tongue had forgotten how to make contact with his palate and could do no more than revolve aimlessly in his mouth; All his words came tumbling out in meaningless confusion. He raised his arm, pointed to Banu and said, 'This is my wife. This is Mrs Amin, Mrs Banu Amin, Mrs Bania Amin. Hello Bania darling, meet my dear, dear friends and their beautiful wives. Come on. Oh, come on.' His guests began to laugh and the laughter of their wives became hysterical. Amin supporting himself on the furniture, advanced on Banu, knocking the vases and the pictures off the low tables. He turned to look at his guests as a conjurer looks at his audience just before he produces a pigeon from a hat. His eyes were turned upwards and he was biting his lips. Suddenly he pulled Banu's stole away and tried to throw it to the floor, but he overbalanced and fell on a table.

The movement of the stole brought Banu's long hair falling over her face, and with a scream she turned round. She moved her hair aside and looked at Amin, and then, hiding her face in both hands she sat huddled as though the loss of her stole had left her whole body naked.

But the removal of her stole, and the brief interval in which she had moved aside the hair from her face, had intoxicated the guests even more and they began to sing out in her praise, 'Good God! What a masterpiece! Lahore's Ingrid Bergman! Wonderful! Exquisite! Beauty incarnate! The 20th Century Lady Hamilton!'

'Thank you, thank you very much.' Amin acknowledged their praise as four of his guests' wives helped him to rise to his feet.

Banu's well-knit body was shaking convulsively as though someone was repeatedly striking her.

'Don't cry, Bania.' Amin moved towards her on his hands and knees. 'Forgive me darling. Ever since we were married I've ill-treated you. Forgive me. I'm a sinner. I'm a criminal. I'm a bastard. Forgive me Bania. From today your purdah is at an end—by God, from this very day, from this very moment, as God is my witness, as my seniors are my witnesses, as my seniors' wives are my witnesses. All of you are witnesses, aren't you?'

'Yes!' they all shouted.

'So be happy now, Bania darling.' And then God knows what happened to him, but Amin's voice choked. His face was twitching. He began to laugh and to cry at the same time. And then he said, 'It was to celebrate this that I drank. You drink too. Call the servant and give him a drink. Give everybody a drink. Shake hands with my officers. Dance the *luddi* for them. Do something to please

them, Bania darling. Oh, Bania darling!' And Amin fell at the feet
of the shrinking Banu and began to laugh and cry like a child.

Further Reading

Scarcely any of Qasmi's stories have been translated into English.
The Unwanted, translated by Khalid Hassan is included in *Nothing
But the Truth: Pakistani Short Stories* (Montreal), Dawson College,
1978.

Strange New World

Kulwant Singh Virk (1921–   )

Translated from the Punjabi by Harbans Singh. From *Land of the Five Rivers: Stories from the Punjab,* edited by Khushwant Singh and Jaya Thadani (Bombay), Jaico Books, 1965

Those who choose to write in Punjabi are mainly from the Sikh community. The rural themes popular in Punjabi literature tend to give it more of a regional quality than the literature of other languages. Punjabi speakers in Pakistan seem not to write in Punjabi but prefer Urdu.

Sikhs from the Punjab have often had to leave their native villages to seek their fortune in the city or even across the seas—as the presence of Sikh communities as far afield as Hong Kong, Vancouver, Nairobi and Southall testifies. Partition affected them brutally along with other Punjabis— Hindus, Muslims and other creeds as well as Sindhis and Bengalis. But migration to new places did not demoralise the Sikh families as much as others and one of the interesting features of post-Independence India was the initiative and skill shown by the displaced Sikh farmers in rebuilding their lives.

Virk is one of the best-known post-Independence generation of Punjabi writers, having had some five collections of stories published. Uprooting and starting anew is the theme of much of his work. The present story is an amusing and touching variation on this theme.

How Hazara Singh made a comfortable living without putting his hand to tilling or any other conventional mode of occupation was a mystery to many in the village. But those who knew, never tired of admiring his unusual skill at cattle rustling or house-breaking, and of relating stories of his nightly adventures.

In children's books, thieves generally end up locked behind impregnable prison bars. But Hazara Singh had never been to jail. In fact, he was not even among those acknowledged miscreants whom the police inspector, on his occasional visits to the village, would summon and openly beat up in our school compound, by way of routine chastisement.

The visit of the Inspector, who always camped in our school, meant a holiday for us. But we did not stir out of doors for fear of the police. We only listened, all agog, from the roofs of our houses, to the yells and cries of the criminals coming from the school grounds.

On such occasions, Hazara Singh, in his immaculate white turban, would sit chatting with the police chief on the string *charpoy,* or he would be seen busily running around making arrangements for the officer's accommodation and hospitality.

Whatever little land Hazara Singh possessed was cultivated by his tenants and he seemed to lead a life unburdened by any visible care or responsibility. Other peasants clad themselves in coarse home-spun and could only afford, on rare festive occasions, to wear clothes bought from town. Hazara Singh always wound round his head a respectable length of fine muslin and had an ample amount of machine-woven white calico loosely draped round his waist.

Apparently opulent, Hazara Singh would frequently be seen visiting his friends or relations in the neighbouring villages. In his own village he sat among the elders and was always the central figure in such gatherings. He could talk of various things and, as a born raconteur, was full of anecdotes and stories which held his listeners entranced.

I loved to hear Hazara Singh talk, especially of his daring exploits. Whenever I was home on holiday from my school in town, I spent long hours listening to his tales which were told with humour and graphic descriptions. He was proud of his skills in rustling and house-breaking but from his accounts it was not difficult to guess that he relished the former more and got a greater sense of triumph from stealing cattle. It was like a military operation in which many of the enemy's troops were rounded up. Whenever we sat together he would start to reminisce.

'One day my nephew came to me,' he said, sitting on a tree stump and scratching the earth with a twig, 'and said that he needed a pair of bullocks. He had seen a pair which belonged to the Chathas of Ajnianwala and he wanted me somehow to deliver them to his farm! I told him that the Chathas were his father's friends and that he would not be able to keep the bullocks if they were ever traced to him. And if he was ultimately going to be compelled to return the animals why must he expose me to the rigours of mounting the operation on a cold wintry night? But he insisted and assured me that I could count on his ability to keep the animals once I had managed to pass them on to him. I promised I would.

'It was no easy task stealing those animals. They were the finest and the cleverest pair I had ever encountered. They would be startled by the slightest shadow and once frightened it was very difficult to catch hold of them. The rows of jingling bells round their necks could raise the alarm.

'I had, of course, taken with me two handfuls of green fodder. Sniffing food in my lap the animals were not scared. Instead, they stretched their heads towards me. Caressing them affectionately I removed the bells from their necks and walked out quietly with the two animals following me. They were a well-known pair in that part of the country and anybody within a radius of nine or ten miles would have recognised them at once. I had taken a fast mare with me and rode off with the bullocks tied by a rope to the saddle. Really good oxen will always follow a galloping horse. By sunrise I had done more than twenty miles and reached Ranike village in time to wish my cousins an early "good morning". I tied the animals in a sugar-cane field and lay down to rest on the charpoy. At nightfall I set out for my nephew's farm and got there before daybreak.

'The owners, however, had been following close on my heels. It wasn't difficult to keep track of three fleeing animals and the next day they also arrived at my nephew's. They knew for certain where their bullocks were and had brought many friends to back them up. My nephew at last gave in and returned the animals. I still get annoyed about it and ask him why he made me ride through two cold nights if he didn't have the guts to keep them.'

Rustling was exciting but there was more money in house-breaking and Hazara Singh was no less proficient at it. His first principle was to avoid noise at all cost and he had devised a variety of techniques. Cloth, he had found, was the best sound absorbent and any object likely to make a noise had to be covered with it. The villages around he had classified into two distinct categories—'his own' and 'the others'. He would never dream of doing anything in the first but had no qualms about the latter. But it was difficult to say which set of villages was dearer to him. He knew them all: the roads and lanes, bushes and pastures, canals and streams. Just as a bee that flits from one flower to another sipping nectar considers the whole garden her own, so Hazara Singh loved both sets of villages.

Hazara Singh was proud of his skill and he made no secret of it. Not many people, he reckoned, could work with such speed and dexterity. 'The moneylenders of Mangewala had a *pukka* built house,' he told us once. 'The outer walls were plastered over with cement and were thought to be impregnable. One day I heard that the moneylenders had come into a good bit of crisp money from some mortgaged land they had released. This was my big chance. There were four of us and with four men sleeping in the front of the house we had to work at the back. I knew it wouldn't be easy to dig through the walls so I decided to cut into the foundations. We kept digging away until the early hours of the morning and managed to worm our way right into the house. We collected whatever we could lay our hands on and made a quick getaway. Next day the police inspector came and visited the spot. I was also present. He examined the tunnel and praised the thief who had dug it for his ingenuity and labour. He said he would compliment the man— after he had caught him.'

House-breaking was a sport for Hazara Singh—a sport which was exciting because of its risks. 'You can never tell if you'll be able to escape the way you came in,' he would say. 'Of course, I could hold off three or four men as I can run and wield a stick as well as anyone else. But it's always a cat-and-mouse game, you know.

'Once, three of us entered a village under cover of darkness. Two of us started cutting through a wall while the third stood look-out round the corner. The wretch dozed off, but we carried on with our work, relying on him to warn us if anything went wrong. Meanwhile, someone in the village saw us and went to get help. As I was creeping into the tunnel we had dug, I heard dogs barking and saw a crowd of people blocking our exit to the street. They thought that was our only escape route but I worked it out differently. Instead of backing out into the street we went into the house, jumped over the wall into another house and by repeating this operation a few times, escaped successfully. Later, the villagers came to know of it and teased me whenever we met. "So you nearly robbed our rich neighbours," they said to me and I had to admit that it would have been all up for me if I had been caught that night. All a question of luck!'

Then came Partition and the land of five rivers was torn in two. Hazara Singh had to leave the villages he had loved, the farms and fields, the canals and highways of which he knew every square inch. He had to trudge his weary way with a caravan of refugees over the border to Karnal. This, too, was Punjab, he was told, and here, too, there were villages and houses, farms and canals. But how different it all was! How could this environment, so dull and uninspiring, ever be 'home' he thought.

After a few weeks I also arrived there. I had been looking forward to meeting Hazara Singh. He was for me the only stable element in that changing, crumbling world. He surely would be the same—brave, resourceful and adventurous. I was wrong. Hazara Singh, like the rest of us, had become uprooted and lost.

'It hardly makes any difference to you, Uncle,' I said to him one day with the blindness of youth. 'You're like government officers, the same here as over there, aren't you?'

'How can that be, son?' he asked quietly. 'Am I any different from my brothers? Do I not share in their sorrows and trials?'

'That's true, but if one possesses an art like yours then surely one can cash in on it anywhere, can't one?'

'Oh, you mean that! Well no, not really. Far from it.' Hazara Singh shook his head sadly. 'My steps are not firm upon this ground, they waver. How can I do anything here? One needs the sights and sounds of home, the faces of kinsmen and friends. Here,' he repeated, 'I can do nothing.'

Neither danger nor fear of the law had ever deterred Hazara Singh, but a strange new world defeated him.

Further Reading

The Bull Beneath the Earth, a sentimental tale of Punjabi soldiers and their heroism in the Second World War is included in *Contemporary Indian Short Stories,* Vol. II (New Delhi), Sahitya Akademi, 2nd ed. 1977.

For stories by other Punjabi writers see:

Land of the Five Rivers edited by Khushwant Singh and Jaya Thadani (Bombay), Jaico Books, 1965

A Death in Delhi

Kamleshwar (1932–   )

Translated from the Hindi by Gordon C. Roadarmel. From *A Death in Delhi: Modern Hindi Short Stories,* translated and edited by G. Roadarmel (Berkeley), University of California Press, 1972. The original was written in 1963.

Kamleshwar is a modern Hindi writer who is concerned with social issues. His stories look at the individual in a social context and examine the problems of modern society—alienation, sexual guilt and weakening family ties.

Kamleshwar's literary skill and his use of telling detail which can build up a picture in the manner of the Impressionists, provides an evocative background to his stories. Born in Uttar Pradesh and educated at Allahabad University, he knows the world he writes about and in *Summer Days,* for example, the dust and heat of a north Indian summer in a small town has never seemed more real.

In the present story, the narrator is trying hard to ignore his moral obligation to attend a funeral. In contrast to this is the attitude of his neighbours, whose absence of grief is symbolic of the dislocation of human values.

A shroud of fog covers everything. It is past nine in the morning, but all of Delhi is enmeshed in the haze. The streets are damp. The trees are wet. Nothing is clearly visible. The bustle of life reveals itself in sounds, sounds which fill the ears. Sounds are coming from every part of the house. As on other days, Vaswani's servant has lit the stove and it can be heard sizzling beyond the wall. In the adjoining room, Atul Mavani is polishing his shoes. Upstairs, the Sardarji* is putting Fixo on his moustache. Behind the curtain on his window a bulb gleams like an immense pearl. All the doors are closed and all the windows are draped, but throughout the building there is the clamour of life. On the third floor, Vaswani has closed the bathroom door and turned on the tap.

Buses are rushing through the fog, the whine of the heavy tyres approach and then fade into the distance. Motor rickshaws are dashing along recklessly. Somebody had just flipped down a taxi-meter. The phone is ringing at the doctor's place next door, and some girls heading for work are passing through the back alley.

The cold is intense. On the shivering streets, cars and buses, their horns blaring, slash through the clouds of fog. The pavements are crowded but each person, wrapped in fog, seems like a drifting wisp of cotton. Those wisps of cotton advance silently into the sea of haze. The buses are crowded. People huddle on the cold seats amidst figures hanging like Jesus from the cross—arms outstretched to the icy handrails of the bus.

In the distance, a funeral procession is coming down the street. This must be the funeral I just read about in the newspaper, 'The death of Seth Diwanchand, the renowned and beloved Karolbagh business magnate, occurred this evening at Irwin Hospital. His body has been taken to his home. Tomorrow morning at nine o'clock the funeral will proceed by way of Arya Samaj Road to Panchkuin cremation ground for the last rites.' This must be his bier coming up the street now. Walking silently and slowly behind it are some people, wrapped in mufflers and wearing hats. Nothing can be seen very clearly.

There is a knock at my door. I put the paper aside and open the door. Atul Mavani is standing there. 'I've a problem, friend. No one showed up today to do the ironing. Can I use your iron?' Atul's words are a relief. I was afraid he might raise the question of joining the funeral procession. I immediately give him the iron, satisfied that he plans to iron his trousers and then set off on a round of the foreign embassies.

Ever since reading about Seth Diwanchand's death in the paper I've been apprehensive that someone will show up to suggest I join the funeral. Everyone in this building was acquainted with him, and they are all genteel, sophisticated people.

The Sardarji's servant comes down the stairs noisily, opens the door and starts to go out. 'Dharma! Where are you going?' I call out, hoping for reassurance.

When he answers, 'To buy butter for the Sardarji,' I quickly hold out the money for him to get me some cigarettes at the same time.

The Sardarji is sending out for butter for his breakfast, which means that he is not planning to join the funeral procession either. I am further relieved. Since Atul Mavani and the Sardarji are not planning to go, it's out of the question for me. Those two and the Vaswani family visited Seth Diwanchand's place more than I did. I only met the man four or five times. If they are not planning to attend, then there's surely no question of my having to go.

Mrs Vaswani has appeared on the front balcony. There is a strange pallor on her attractive face, and a touch of redness from the lipstick she wore last evening. She is wearing just a dressing gown and is fastening up her hair. 'Darling,' her voice rings out, 'bring me some toothpaste, please.'

I'm further reassured. The Vaswanis must not be attending the rites either.

Far down on Arya Samaj Road, the funeral procession is slowly approaching.

Atul Mavani comes to return the iron. After taking it, I want to close the door but he comes in and says, 'Did you hear that Seth Diwanchand died yesterday?'

'I just read about it in the paper,' I answer blandly, to avoid further discussion of the matter. Atul's face is shining. He must have shaved.

'He was a really fine man, that Diwanchand.'

If the comments go any further there will be a moral obligation for me to join the funeral procession. So I ask, 'What happened about that business of yours?'

'The machine's about to arrive. As soon as it does, I'll get my commission. This commission work is really senseless, but what's to be done? If I can just place eight or ten machines, I'll start my own business.' Atul continues, 'Brother, Diwanchandji helped me a lot when I first came here. It's because of him that I got any work at all. People really respected him.'

My ears prick up at the name, Diwanchand. Then the Sardarji

puts his head out of the window. 'Mr Mavani! What time should we go?'

'Well, the time was given as nine o'clock, but it'll probably be late because of the cold and fog.' This must be a reference to the funeral.

The Sardarji's servant, Dharma, has brought me the cigarettes and is setting out tea on the table upstairs. Then Mrs Vaswani speaks up, 'I think Premila's bound to be there. Don't you think so, darling?'

'Well, she ought to be,' Mr Vaswani replies, crossing the balcony. 'Hurry up and get ready.'

'Will you be going to the Coffee House this evening?' Atul asks me.

'Probably.' I wrap the blanket around me and he goes back to his room.

A moment later he calls out, 'Is the electricity on, brother?'

'Yes it's on.' He must be using an immersion heater.

'Polish!' the shoeshine boy announces politely in his daily fashion, and the Sardarji calls him upstairs. The boy sits outside polishing, while the Sardarji instructs his servant to bring lunch promptly at one o'clock. 'Fry some *papars* and make a salad as well.'

I know the man's servant is a scoundrel. He never serves a meal on time, and doesn't cook what the Sardarji orders.

Thick fog covers the street outside with no sign of sunshine. The man selling wheatcakes and *gram* has come and set up his cart as usual. He is polishing the plates which are rattling.

The number seven bus is leaving with its crucified Christs standing inside, while a conductor sells tickets to people waiting in the queue. Coins jingle each time he returns their change. Among the cotton balls wrapped in haze, the dark-uniformed conductor looks like Satan himself.

And the funeral procession has come a little closer.

'Shall I wear a blue *sari*?' asks Mrs Vaswani.

Vaswani's muffled reply suggests that he is adjusting the knot on his tie.

The servant has brushed the Sardarji's suit and draped it on the hanger. The Sardarji stands in front of the mirror tying his turban.

Atul Mavani reappears, briefcase in hand, wearing the suit made for him last month. His face looks fresh and his shoes are shining. 'Aren't you going?' he asks. Before I can ask, 'Going where?' he calls out, 'Come on, Sardarji. It's getting late—it's past ten o'clock.'

Two minutes later, the Sardarji starts down the stairs. Meanwhile, Vaswani spots Mavani from upstairs and asks, 'Where did you get that suit made?'

'Over in Khan Market.'

'It's very nicely done. I'd like to get the tailor's address from you.' Then he calls to his wife, 'Come on, dear. I'll be waiting for you downstairs.' Joining Mavani and the Sardarji, he feels the suit material. 'Is the lining Indian?'

'English.'

'It fits beautifully,' he says, jotting down the tailor's address. Mrs Vaswani appears on the balcony, looking immaculate in the damp, cold morning. The Sardarji winks at Mavani and starts whistling.

The bier is now directly below my room. A few people are walking with it, engrossed in conversation, and a couple of cars are creeping along.

Mrs Vaswani comes downstairs, a flower in her hair, and the Sardarji adjusts his handerkerchief in his coat pocket. Before they go out of the door, Vaswani asks me, 'Aren't you coming?'

'You go ahead. I'll be right there,' I respond, though unsure where I'm to go.

The funeral has moved down the road. A car comes from behind and slows down near the procession. The driver exchanges a few words with someone walking in the procession, and then the car surges ahead. Two cars following the procession also slip ahead.

I stand watching as Mrs Vaswani and the other three head for the taxi stand. Mrs Vaswani has put on her fur wrap and the Sardarji is either offering her his fur gloves or just displaying them. The taxi driver stops and opens the door and the four of them get in. Now the taxi is heading this way and I can hear laughter inside. Vaswani points towards the procession and tells the driver something.

I stand quietly observing everything, and somehow I feel now as though the least I could have done was to join Diwanchand's funeral procession. I know his son well and at times like this one should offer sympathy even to enemies. The cold outside almost destroys my resolve but the question of joining the funeral keeps needling me.

The taxi slows down near the bier. Mavani sticks his head out and says something. Then the taxi goes round to the right and moves ahead.

Feeling beaten, I put on my overcoat, slip on some sandals, and go down the stairs. My feet propel me automatically towards the procession and I fall in quietly behind the bier. Four men are carrying it on their shoulders, with seven others walking alongside—the seventh being myself. What a difference it makes when a man dies. Just last year, when Diwanchand's daughter was married, there were thousands of guests, and cars were lined up in front of his house.

We have reached Link Road. Around the next turn is the Panchkuin cremation ground.

As the procession turns the corner, I see a crowd of people and a row of cars. There are some scooters also. A chatter of voices comes from a group of women sitting at one side. Each has a different hair style, and they stand around with the same sensuality one sees in Connaught Place.★ Cigarette smoke is rising from the crowd of men and blending into the fog. The red lips and white teeth of the women shine as they talk, and there's arrogance in their eyes . . .

The bier has been set down outside on a platform. Now there is silence. The scattered crowd has gathered round the body, and chauffeurs, holding bouquets and garlands of flowers, wait for a look from their masters.

My eyes fall on Vaswani. He's trying to signal his wife to go over by the corpse, but she keeps standing there talking to another woman. Nearby are the Sardarji and Atul Mavani.

The face of the corpse has been uncovered, and now the women are placing flowers and garlands around it. The chauffeurs, their duty done, stand near their cars, smoking.

One lady, after depositing a garland, takes a handkerchief from her bag, puts it to her eyes, sniffles a little, and then steps back.

Now, all the women have taken out handkerchiefs and there is a sound of nose blowing.

Some of the men have lit incense and set it at the head of the corpse. They stand motionless.

From the sound, increased sadness has apparently reached the hearts of the women.

Atul Mavani takes a paper from his briefcase and is showing it to Vaswani. I think it's his passport application.

Now the bier is being taken inside the cremation ground. The crowd stands outside the gate, watching. The chauffeurs have either finished their cigarettes or put them out, and stand guard by their cars.

The bier has gone inside now.

The people who come to offer condolences are beginning to leave. One can hear car doors opening and closing. The scooters start up and some people are heading towards the bus stop on Reading Road.

The fog is still thick. Buses are passing by and Mrs Vaswani says, 'Premila has invited us over this evening. You'll come along, won't you, dear? There'll be a car for us. That's all right, isn't it?'

Vaswani nods his head in agreement.

The women leaving by car are smiling and saying goodbye to each other. The cars start off . . .

Atul Mavani and the Sardarji are walking towards the bus stop. If I were properly dressed, I could go straight to work from here. But it's already eleven-thirty.

The pyre has been lit and four or five men are seated on a bench underneath a tree. Like me, they just happened to come along inside. They must be taking the day off. Otherwise they would have come ready to go on to work.

I can't decide whether to return home, clean up and then go to the office, or whether to use the excuse of a death to take the day off. After all, there was a death and I did join the funeral procession.

Further Reading

A few of Kamleshwar's short stories, translated into English, can be found in the following anthologies:

Hindi Short Stories translated by Shrawan Kumar and Prabhakar Machwe (Bombay), Jaico Books, 1970

Stories from India ed. Khushwant Singh and Qurrutulain Hyder (New Delhi), Sterling Paperbacks, 1974

Modern Indian Short Stories ed. Suresh Kohli (New Delhi), Arnold/Heinemann, 1974

Baby Deer

Sunil Gangopadhyaya (1934–   )

Translated from the Bengali by Ranjana Ash. From *Selected Stories of Sunil Gangopadhyaya* (Calcutta), Indian International, 1972

Born in 1934 in Faridpur, now in Bangladesh, and educated in Calcutta, Gangopadhyaya is one of the most brilliant poets writing in Bengali today. His popularity, however, is due more to his fiction and, in particular, his short stories which are widely read. While many of his stories deal with intellectuals, generally not very affluent but terribly articulate and analytical about their quest for freedom of expression, others are written from a more radical viewpoint about such basic issues as hunger and survival. His stories, set in the tribal areas of Bihar, such as *Baby Deer* and his novel, *Days and Nights in the Forest,* filmed some years ago by Satyajit Ray, bring out pointedly the contrast between the educated, well-to-do tourists and the hungry tribal people who, despite their poverty, seem to possess something of the free spirit that eludes the former. Gangopadhyaya's style is a blend of irony a and poetic eye for detail.

Two or three children sit silently on the veranda steps. They neither ask for anything, nor do they talk among themselves but sit staring in silence. Pitch black in colour, ages ranging from ten to twelve, a loincloth masquerading as a *dhoti;* the only girl among them reminds me of Audrey Hepburn in a vague sort of way. She is an Oraon or Munda★ girl of ten or eleven who cannot possibly be the least bit like Audrey Hepburn, yet there is something about her face which reminds one of the actress. Perhaps that is why I feel sorry for her and also, probably, my conscience which prompts me to let them stay. Nevertheless, we feel ill at ease as we sit on the veranda of the *dak bungalow* at Netarhat, facing an enormous valley and the majestic splendour of the sun. Subimal, his wife Aruna, his sister-in-law Baruna, and I are embarrassed as we eat our breakfast in front of these dirty children sitting on the steps. Ever since we arrived here the day before yesterday, they have been with us all the time.

In the gravel-covered yard in front of the dak bungalow is a dog, a rather nice-looking dog—the sort of big, shaggy-haired mongrel you can find in hill stations. It sits perched like the dog on the gramophone records, as if waiting for someone. I don't like eating the crust and throw it into the air. The dog jumps and catches it in its mouth and the children follow my hands as I throw the bits of toast right up to the dog's mouth.

The wind blows tremulously and the cold feels good, especially when one remembers how they are suffering from the heat down in Calcutta. The clouds fly over like mist. One wonders whether they can really be clouds as there has been no rain in these parts for almost two years. Yet there seem to be clouds rushing around the hill tops every day. Aruna's hand slipped carelessly as she was eating her egg and a blob of yolk fell on her *sari*. Quickly she tried to wipe it off with a wet handkerchief. She was obviously annoyed and said irritably, 'It would be better if we had breakfast inside. How can anybody eat if people keep staring at them?'

Baruna did not agree. 'But why should we waste such a beautiful morning sitting indoors? These people turn up everywhere. Can't the authorities do something to keep the tourist spots, at least, free of beggars?'

Subimal had finished his breakfast. Lighting a cigarette he said, somewhat detached, 'Most probably these aren't beggars, just local people. Conditions here are very bad right now.'

The yolk had congealed and Aruna could not get it off. Still annoyed she said, 'Government's become so useless, whether it's left or right.' She then took two slices of toast from her own plate and one each from Baruna's and mine and offered them to the children. 'Come here, come here. Take this and go away.'

The children looked at one another, then one of them came forward, hesitant and shy. He took the four slices and shared them out among themselves. They were very well-mannered as they lowered their heads and began to eat noiselessly.

Subimal laughed and in indulgent tones asked his wife, 'But how long will you be able to feed these kids?'

The dog growled softly and came forward. Now Aruna had to

smile. 'It's your turn now, is it? Come along then and take this.' She threw the last slice of toast from Baruna's plate to the dog. It ran, gobbled it up in a second and then resumed its gramophone-like pose.

Baruna said, 'But they haven't gone.'

The children were still sitting on the steps, looking at us. I wanted to tease Baruna and said, 'That's the joke: we don't mind a dog watching us eat but let another human being do it and we hate it.'

Baruna got cross as I had hoped she might. She looked at me disdainfully and said, 'Now I suppose you're going to start lecturing us as if we were the guilty ones. Just because these people can't get anything to eat are we supposed to starve?'

'At least *you* should, considering how blooming you look!'

'And what about you? Don't *you* ever look at yourself in the mirror?'

Why should *I* look in a mirror when I can see my reflection in your eyes?'

'Now you're going too far. If you keep on at me like this I shan't stay. I'll go away today by myself.'

Subimal and Aruna began to laugh. I said, 'But you can't do that. You and I are supposed to be going to the watch tower this afternoon. Don't you remember you promised to only yesterday.'

'Rubbish! You *do* tell lies. I'll never go alone with you.'

'In that case you won't be able to go at all. You don't know the rules of the place. People can only go in twos to the tower.'

'Nonsense! There aren't such rules but even if there are, I'll go with Jamaibabu.'*

'But will Subimal let his wife come with me?'

In mock seriousness Subimal said that he certainly would not. At this Aruna curled her lips and nudged her husband, 'My, my!'

Baruna, with all the earnestness of a seventeen-year-old said, 'But she doesn't have to. First I'll go with Jamaibabu, then he'll go with Didi, then you and he or else you and . . .'

'When Didi and Jamaibabu go up and you are left with me, it'll be like the tiger, the goat and the bag of hay. Do you know the story?'

Baruna moved her chair away making a lot of noise. 'I haven't got time for this sort of thing.' Then, directing her anger at the children, she cried out in a shrill voice, 'Go away at once. Stop bothering us all the time.'

I smiled. 'I know how to get rid of them. Do you want to see?'

I took a note from my pocket and called out, 'Children, can you buy cigarettes anywhere?'

They looked at one another. Then one of them said, 'Yes, sahib, at the Co-operative.'

I produced an empty cigarette packet. 'Bring me four packets like this and I'll give all four of you ten *paise baksheesh*. No, Audrey Hepburn will get fifteen paise.'

Aruna looked surprised. 'Audrey Hepburn?'

I laughed. 'Doesn't she look like Audrey Hepburn? Look at her eyes.'

Baruna burst out laughing. 'Oh dear! You're going to give Audrey Hepburn charity. What cheek!'

'Not charity, but payment for work.'

'We'll see how many times you have to send them to buy cigarettes.'

We had lunch in the dining room that day. The dak bungalow Muslim cook was really good and had made a lovely *biriani* and chicken roast.

There was not much heat in the sun that day. It was a day of gentle wind and shade. To be alive on days like this is sheer delight. Baruna did not want to stay in. At seventeen she was restless to go out and see things. The patterns of light and shade on the distant mountains kept on changing and the far extended valley, though seen every day, never got stale. It was only natural that on days like these Baruna, who was on holiday, should want to go out. Subimal had been married for three years but he made excuses to stay in with Aruna. So after tea I went out for a walk with Baruna.

We walked along a path in the forest to the watch tower. The view from the tower of the hills and the forest was one beautiful vastness. The only objects one could see were trees but they were withering in the sun. This year they had no new leaves. And the river bed in the forest was dry. Everywhere were signs of the drying-up that comes with the failure of the rains. Patches of land, where the jungles had been cleared for cultivation on the slopes of the hills, could be seen in the distance. The rice and maize growing there were waiting to die. Yet, my imagination was such that I tried to find beauty even in the midst of such dessication.

There was only one source of water. It was the reservoir that provided the dak bungalow's water supply and also probably the local school's. As far as the eye could see this was the only source of water was obviously maintained with considerable trouble. The thumping of the pumps could be heard continuously.

Baruna had said, 'How pretty! A hill-top lake! We must go and sit by it one afternoon. Aren't there any wild animals in the forest?'

I said, 'Of course. Haven't you read about the tigers of Palamau? I've heard that there are elephants and many kinds of deer.'

'Wouldn't it be fun if we could see a tiger from here?'

I let out a wild yell. 'Here's a tiger right beside you.'

Baruna gave me a push in mock anger. 'My! What powerful lungs!' Then looking below the watch tower she became really angry. 'They've come here as well. They'll drive us mad. I'm really fed up.'

The same three or four children were standing at the foot of the tower, gazing at us from below. They neither spoke, nor made any sort of noise.

Baruna said, 'Do they suppose we've come here to eat? Why must they keep following us around everywhere?'

I placed my hand gently on her shoulder and, in a voice full of concern, asked, 'Why are you getting so worked up about it? You don't have to look at them. There are so many beautiful things to see. Come let's look at them together.'

'I simply can't do that. Always staring at us like starving people. What do you think they keep looking at? Do we keep on eating all the time? It was only this morning that you gave them some money.'

'They haven't come to beg. Perhaps they like looking at us. Just as we've come to see the mountains, wide skies, forest, so they've come to fill their eyes with our beautiful clothes, our beautiful food. To look at us should certainly make them feel good! They're not supposed to appreciate the beauty of the forests and hills!'

'You may be right but I think it's awful. Isn't anybody meant to go on holiday? And if while enjoying themselves people have to put up with this sort of thing . . .'

'When on holiday it's best to close one's eyes to some things. To derive enjoyment means parting with a few cherished possessions, getting rid of one or two dearly held notions. You're still very young so you can't understand. Of course, it's important to travel and have a good time. But if we remember the starving millions then everything will be spoilt. So you must put all that behind you. See how we grown-ups can so easily forget such things. Just a few paise baksheesh and that's that!'

She looked upset and sounded annoyed. 'I can't bear it any longer! I sometimes wish I could give them a good hiding.'

On the way back, the children trailed us to the dak bungalow and sat down on the steps silently, asking for nothing. Some new members had now joined the group.

One gets hungrier in the cold weather and we had walked a lot. The result was that we finished dinner very quickly. As the dining-room curtain waved in the breeze eight or nine children could be seen through the gap. I sat with my back to them. While sipping coffee, Subimal embarked on his south Indian travelogue. When that ended we began discussing our finances and whether we could include a trip to McCluskygunj from Netarhat.

The next afternoon we filled our flasks with tea and set off for the reservoir. The ducks of Manas Sarovar* evidently knew all about the lake for a flock of them were swimming in the water in rows looking like the strings of a many-layered necklace. One side of the reservoir embankment was high. It was surprising to find such a big water tank on the top of a hill. They must have excavated really deep with machines to find water.

Subimal began to coax Aruna to give us a song and Aruna, full of excuses, was trying to refuse. She had a sore throat ever since she had eaten the sour yogurt in Ranchi; to sing on an empty stomach could mean sliding from one key to another—a very bad thing for one's voice. In order that I should not have to listen to Aruna's singing, I kept on thinking up all sorts of conversational gambits.

Baruna did not sing but was taking dancing lessons at Uday Shankar's school. I wondered whether I could tease her by asking her to dance for us up here. She was not paying attention to us but picking up little pebbles and throwing them into the water.

Only two of the children were still with us. The girl and one of the boys were sitting quietly some distance away. They had certainly never begged from us. If we ever gave them anything they would take it but they never asked us for food. They would merely sit, quite still, watching us.

Suddenly Subimal said, 'Sunil, You're quite right. That girl does resemble Audrey Hepburn. Her eyes are beautiful.'

Aruna said, 'Poor things! One does feel sorry for them but what can we do? One feels bad but how much food could we possibly give them? Little girl, come here.'

The girl remained sitting while continuing to look at us. Aruna called out again, 'Little girl, come here. Come here. Don't be afraid.'

The girl now got up and came towards Aruna very timidly. Aruna took her hand and said, 'What a pretty face. If only she were fair, but black isn't bad.'

As she was saying this she turned towards her husband whose complexion is almost like mine. Subimal declaimed in very lofty tones, 'Black is beautiful!'

At this point something strange happened. Baruna suddenly began to whisper excitedly, 'Look, look, what's that? Is it a kid or a fawn? It's a baby deer!'

We all turned to look and saw a fawn standing not very far from us, and looking in our direction. It was not very dark yet, and in the clear light of the evening we saw it edging, step by step, towards the reservoir. We were looking intently at it when Baruna whispered in my ear, 'Isn't it beautiful? It's so near. Can't we catch it? I can take it to Calcutta and keep it as a pet.'

Because Audrey Hepburn was behind Subimal she had not seen the deer at first but when she did she yelled in some incomprehensible language. Till then I had not heard her utter a single word and I could not have imagined her producing such piercing sounds. Still yelling she began to run. The deer, frightened by her cries, was backing away into the field but surprisingly it did not go very far. It stood motionless for a moment and then began edging near us again, one foot at a time. I was amazed by the animal's behaviour. Why was it so anxious to come close to human beings?

Subimal's voice was sad. 'Poor thing! It'll be dead by the end of the day.'

Baruna screamed, '*Dead*? It's going to die? Why?'

Can't you tell? It's come up here to look for water. There's no water anywhere in the forest. Probably it hasn't had a drop of water for the last three or four days. Didn't you notice how unsteadily it ran? Was that the swiftness of a deer? It's dying.'

In a voice choking with emotion, Baruna said, 'It's going to drink water. Let's go away and then it can come to the water's edge. Come.'

'Do you think that if we move aside it'll be able to drink? Its life is ebbing away. How sad! And a rare species of deer too—spotted deer.'

Subimal's prophecy did not take long to come true. Some eight or nine children came rushing along with that girl. There was a small stick in each of their hands and two of them had bows and arrows. The deer was now by the reservoir embankment. But they gave it such a fright that it ran towards the clearing full of shrubs and bushes. The children could see it quite clearly and chased after it in hot pursuit, yelling.

Baruna wailed, 'They're going to kill the deer. Sunilda, please stop them. Oh no! How beautiful and tender it looks. Sunilda, please go and catch it.'

As if she was asking me to get her a golden hind I simply said, 'Don't be silly, as if a deer can ever be caught.'

'Then stop them killing it.'

'As if they'll listen to me.'

We saw the entire tableau like a movie. The deer, terribly weak, could scarcely run. The children were hurling stones and sticks at it. The deer stumbled, hit by a stone, then it got up, ran a few paces before an arrow pierced its neck. It fell flat, shaking in agony and, with the arrow stuck in it, tried to run again. But by then the children had caught up with it. Two of them began beating it with their sticks until its violent jerkings ceased. The whole business did not take more than five minutes.

Aruna spoke. 'How dreadful! Just think it was alive only a minute ago. How entreatingly it looked at the water! Come, let's go back to the bungalow.'

But Subimal said, 'Let's wait a bit and see what happens.'

'No, come on. Runi is such a baby. She can't stand this sort of thing. Darling, there's nothing to cry about.'

Baruna turned her head away. 'I'm not crying.'

'If you're not crying you should wipe your eyes. Really, it's a sin to witness such sights. Come, come we must go away.'

Baruna wiped her eyes with her sari but her voice was stern. 'No, I won't go yet.'

Subimal put his arm on her shoulder and said gently, 'My Runi baby's feeling very sad, isn't she? Don't let it upset you so, dear. Think how happy the children are. After ages they're going to get enough to eat—and meat at that. To find such happiness, things have to be sacrificed at times. It's because you actually saw it all happening that you're feeling awful, but supposing you didn't know anything about it and got a bit of the venison.'

The children's joy knew no bounds. Dragging the deer to the embankment they were practically dancing. The deer's head was lolling on one side, deep red blood spurting out of its mouth. Perhaps a vestige of life remained. The girl took an arrow and dug it into the animal's belly to clean out its entrails. How her smile sparkled then! They were discussing something animatedly. I guessed they were not too anxious to take the deer back to the village where they would have to share it with many others. They were gathering branches and twigs right on the spot and set about making a fire.

We sat on the parapet watching them. Gradually the evening grew dark and the fire glowed bright. They began roasting the deer, turning it round and round. Baruna, her chin resting on her knees, gazed intently at the deer's velvety skin getting charred. The children could not wait. Every few minutes, shouting excitedly, they cut a little piece off and nibbled at it to see if it was ready to eat.

I told Subimal that we should really go home. 'If we keep on staring at them when it's time for them to eat they'll probably feel uncomfortable.'

Subimal agreed. 'Quite right. Let's go. It smells delicious. My mouth's watering.'

Further Reading

Very few of Gangopadhyaya's many short stories, novels and poetry have been translated into English.

The Man who Wanted to be Free from *New Writing in India* edited by A. Jussawalla (London), Penguin, 1974 is about an alienated young man.

One of his novels, *The Adversary,* is available in a translation by Enakshi Chatterjee (New Delhi), Orient Paperbacks, 1974. (It deals with the theme of unemployment among university graduates.)

Monsoon

Burhanuddin Jahangir (1935–)

Translated from the Bengali by Ranjana Ash. From the author's collection
of short stories, *Abichchinna* (Dacca), Samkal Prakashni, 1960

One of the well-known writers of East Pakistan, now Bangladesh,
Jahangir's short stories are mainly about city dwellers, drawn from the
lower-middle class of Dacca.

This story about the frustrations of an unemployed university graduate
represents a major problem throughout the subcontinent where
unemployment keeps rising. The tensions in the family as the son ceases to
respect his parents, are one more manifestation of social change.

It began to rain at seven in the evening and with the rain came the
wind that so often accompanies the monsoons. Shaukat was still in
bed in the sitting room. The rain was coming in through the
window and drops fell on his closed eyelids. He was once again
savouring his favourite dream.

Men cherish dreams but they come to nothing. Shaukat had been
unemployed for a year and now there was the possibility of a job.
He'd had his interview and was waiting for the result. Shaukat had
never, in his blackest moments, imagined that things would turn
out this way. He had thought that when he graduated from the
university he would get a reasonable position with a salary of
around five hundred rupees a month. There would be a house in a
quiet road, a piano in the sitting room and two fair hands resting on
it. The peace and quiet of his hoped-for future had been tarnished
by the dust of time. A question which kept churning inside him was
why a government which had the power to provide employment
but could not, should remain in office. However, just as the earth's
tremendous pressure transforms molten lava into solid rock, so the
burning anxiety of accumulated frustration had hardened within

him. In any case, someone who had remained unemployed for a whole year and who was dependent on an old father for every morsel of rice could not indulge in such daydreams. Merely to survive should be enough for him. But, thought Shaukat, must his survival be just like that of the common herd?

When the dreams he had cherished turned out to be worthless it did not make it any easier to accept the harsh realities of life. Outsiders might regard him as somebody of little worth and no identity to call his own but what about his mother and father? If they had expressed their regret openly, Shaukat might not have been as hurt as he was by their constant, unvarying silence. It was this unspoken criticism that kept needling him. At one stage he had almost come to accept his parents view that one's social worth was higher if one could stick at any sort of job rather than make do with none. But today, the possibility of getting work after such a long time seemed to have cleared the mirror of his hopes of the dust and cobwebs and revealed the dream he had kept hidden for so long.

But had he really hidden it? Something had happened yesterday while the rain was falling noisily, incessantly. They were talking on the veranda. His mother had said, 'Did you know Khoka's* got a job?'

'Where? In which office?' It was Putul's mother, a woman approaching middle age and declining health for which she blamed her husband who had fathered her many children. The sight of them irritated her and her bitterness found eloquent expression.

'If only my eldest boy were like yours. But you didn't mention the name of the firm.'

'Whatever is its name? I just can't remember.'

Putul's mother repeated her question. She was not going to be satisfied until she had found out everything. 'How much will he be making? Have you heard?'

His mother's voice rose. 'As if I wouldn't. He'll start at a hundred and fifty and after he's been made permanent, it'll go up to two hundred.'

'Won't Shuku brother give us a treat?' Putul asked.

His mother caressed her with affection. 'Of course, he will, but first let him become permanent.'

Putul's mother had lowered her voice, but the gist of her words was quite clear. 'Sister,' she said, 'now you'll have to get him married. Since he's started earning it won't look nice if you don't arrange a marriage for him. There are so many girls among our own circle of friends and acquaintances. My Zakia is now in the seventh form.'

As he pictured the scene, Shaukat was filled with disgust. A son's achievement is a mother's pride, and a son in employment means a mother's peace of mind. But it did not become his mother to discuss her lucky son's future with the wife of the stamp vendor in the collector's office and certainly not to become her confidante. How could Putul's mother even consider her daughter as his bride when there was such a gulf between their social positions? Did they think he would never gain promotion or rise socially!

As for his mother: couldn't she speak more softly? Must she shout like a common bazaar woman! Looking at her, sitting with her legs spread out, stuffing *paan* into her mouth and talking loudly, Shaukat could have died for shame. As if nobody else in their neighbourhood had ever got a job; as if it was necessary to announce the news of his employment with a roll of drums like low-class rubbish!

The window slammed shut in a sudden gust of wind. Shaukat's dream was submerged in the water leaking through the cracks in the ceiling.

The rain, which had been pouring throughout the night, had finally got tired and stopped in the morning. His mother was sitting with the dirty pots and pans by the tap. Her white feet were smeared with grime. His father must have finished reading the *Quran* and reciting the morning prayers. He would now be going to wake the two younger boys. 'It's not good to lie abed so late,' he would say in gentle tones.

'Panu, Manu, it's morning. Get up.' He heard his father going round the little courtyard a few times. 'Panu, Manu, aren't you getting up?'

After this they could not remain in bed and had to get up. He could hear their footsteps and then their laughter by the tap.

Then his father came over towards Shaukat's bed. He cleared his throat but unlike other days he did not say anything for a moment. Then in a coaxing voice, 'Khoka, how much longer are you going to sleep? Getting up late can't help anybody to get ahead.'

Shaukat made no response and lay still. Keeping his eyes closed he could ignore his father's presence. Indeed, he felt rather pleased with his pretence. On what could be the most fortunate day of his life his father was still acting as his guardian and that vexed him. Certainly other people also had guardians who comforted them in their time of sorrow. But what about his father? He had always risen with the *koel* but what had he ever achieved in life? Why shouldn't he be annoyed with his father? Till now, everything in Shaukat's life—good and bad, when to pull in the reins, when to let go, the poverty and the humiliation—had been in this man's hands. The realisation of this made Shaukat's entire body shudder in disgust. Not one fragment of his ideal could Shaukat find embodied in his father. The resentment had been building up inside of him for a long time until it had begun to scar him, the revulsion he had been nurturing had now become unbearable. Because he was an educated young man with modern ways, his speech was still refined; but it was no longer possible to conceal the fact that he regarded his father with the contempt that someone outside the family might feel.

His father knew that Shaukat was not asleep. He asked, 'Aren't you going to hear about the interview today?'

'Yes,' he said, opening his eyes.

It was an assistantship in a private firm, a transferable position, where he might get sent off somewhere else at short notice. The manager had been encouraging, as his father well knew, but a lifetime's bitter experience had made him cautious and he wanted to reassure himself. This made Shaukat both angry and nervous.

Mother came into the room with a cup of tea and some puffed rice on a plate. She put it in front of him. 'Here's your breakfast.'

Shaukat took one sip and then said, 'What a dirty cup.'

His mother, embarrassed, replied, 'It got dirty in the rush. I was in such a hurry that it got smeared. Give it to me and I'll wipe it. It's difficult, son, with the kitchen full of cobwebs and soot. I've been asking for it to be decorated . . . .'

But Shaukat did not heed her. 'One doesn't feel like eating when things aren't clean.'

Wiping the cup with her sari, mother said, 'It's only happened this once and you're going on and on about it.'

'Not once but many times,' he wanted to shout at her but he controlled himself. He stared at the sari in silence. It was difficult to tell whether it had been laundered since she had bought it. Dirty clothes were bound to smell! His mother, who had so lovingly and tenderly ráised him since infancy, was dirty—her appearance and behaviour like a washer woman.

She went out stony-faced. She had received a severe blow from a most unexpected quarter. Her son had never behaved like this. He had always stayed in the background, submerged by the family's many privations and wants. That anyone should even be reminded of his existence was hurtful to him like a bitter poison. When relations visited them he would pretend to be asleep lest they ask him what he was 'doing'. Such a boy had now become so vocal, expressing his likes and aversions, his approval and disapproval openly. All right, if he *did* want to say something let him but not in this manner. Shaukat, who had never complained of anything his mother had done, who would have kept quiet had she fed him dust and ashes, was now criticising her. He knew very well that she was forced to wear dirty clothes because she did not have any clean ones. He was quite aware of the way his two younger brothers had to live. His old father's pension was not enough and the poor man was worn out doing private tuition to get more money. Shaukat knew all this and yet could speak like this to his mother. Her entire being smouldered with swiftly ignited anger but it died down quickly and she withdrew, feeling apprehensive.

Shaukat scrutinised the shirt he had kept under his pillow. Starch and a deeper crease and it might have passed as *dhobi*-washed. An electric iron was out of the question but if they had a coal-iron he could have washed and ironed his own clothes and been able to go places. Without any ready cash he could not keep on begging from his father, and hence no laundry. He was lucky to have had his trousers cleaned. Otherwise he could not have gone out looking like a scarecrow. Looking for work meant meeting important *sahibs* at smart places. One simply could not go looking like a fright. What would people say! His father was an old man, his mother stayed at home and his brothers were still young. If they looked ragged, nobody would mind. But when visitors came to the house and his brothers were wearing torn shirts and his father a shabby jacket, he felt ashamed, even angry, as if he were being humiliated. He failed to understand why, in spite of telling his mother repeatedly to stop the boys, they would come rushing on to the verandah. And could not his father be more retiring? What consolation did he get from parading the family's hardship in front of others?

Shaukat had begun to realise that his very identity was being eroded by life's thousand-and-one difficulties and his beautiful dream fast disappearing. Perhaps it was this that was making everything unbearable.

Putul appeared at the door. He asked her whom she was looking for. She laughed. 'Mother's sent some *ilish* fish cooked the way you like. Where's auntie?' she ran off.

Shaukat sat still, his head bowed. This was his world, full of unpleasant social formalities. Once he got the job, he would go away from here but would he get it?

An hour later the sound of slippers and his father came into the room.

Shaukat said, 'Yes, father.'

His father hesitated and then asked, 'Will you be going out now?'

Shaukat looked annoyed. 'Why?'

'You could get the rations. The boys have gone to school and I'm going to get my tuition salary. When your position's been confirmed you'll have to buy some sweets for your little brothers, to celebrate the good news. If you can . . .'

Shaukat cut in. 'So the ration will have to be bought. Very well.'

Father either did not notice his son's changed manner or ignored it. After a pause he said, 'Why not come with me to Famanullah Sahib's house? He knows your manager. A word from him and the job will be yours. Let's go and meet him.'

Shaukat did not answer. It was obvious that he did not want to go. His father spoke hesitantly. 'You're ashamed of going with me, aren't you?'

Before Shaukat could reply, the old man walked away towards the kitchen, anticipating his son's sullen mood. That his son no longer felt concerned about their domestic problems was quite apparent through his words. He could also guess the reason for this indifference but why couldn't the boy wait till he had got some kind of work before expressing his contempt? As long as a person was unemployed, there was no harm in accepting help from another. And it wasn't good enough going on blaming the government. He was ready to accept the government's weakness for failing to recognise his son's true value and he had no regard for such a government but why couldn't his son take an ordinary job? Didn't *he* have to put up with a miserable salary? Had that diminished *his* usefulness or lowered *his* standing? His son had gone far beyond him in education but the boy was sadly lacking in culture. However, there was no alternative other than to try and avoid the awful truth. It would be impossible to have to admit to a son's contempt for his own father.

Mother was grinding the spices. When she saw her husband she stopped. 'How many *saris* can you give me a year so that I don't have to listen to your son's impertinence? When it comes to giving, there's nobody, but when it's a question of passing rude remarks then it's a free-for-all. What spiteful talk! Why do I wear dirty *saris* and not fresh, clean ones? Your son, if you please, wants to know. My clothes smell! I give him dirty food.'

She looked at her husband and her eyes filled with tears. 'What painful words from one's own flesh and blood! He has absolutely no regard for his own mother.'

Her husband stood silent. The hard, cruel truth had pierced his consciousness like a sharp knife. The son he had raised to manhood was becoming estranged from him. His beliefs and views were probably meaningless to his son but to him they were full of significance and feeling for the past. His son's values and the manner in which he expressed them frightened the father. Yes, frightened him for he could see a future in which his son would deny his very existence, would neglect or ignore everyone in the family and consider his relationship to his father a shameful thing.

He had never thought of relying on his son's salary to support him in his old age. Neither had the boy's mother, most probably. The two of them had only prayed in their hearts that the boy should find work, live happily—no, merely survive. Survival was the vital factor. Everything else followed from it.

That a son should treat his parents with such disrespect, even before he had got work, made the father feel helpless. What would the boy do once he *did* get a job?

He was not apprehensive for himself but for his two young sons and his wife once he was dead. Once, he had taken it for granted that Shaukat would shoulder the responsibility of looking after his mother and brothers. He had not kept Shaukat illiterate but had spent everything he owned on the boy's education. An educated boy was the same as a *lakh* of rupees. If only he could see that the younger boys passed their exams then he would be free of worry. They would be able to stand on their own two feet and if nobody wanted to take care of their widowed mother, so be it. Surely she would be able to feed and clothe herself somehow until her death? But the crux of all his anxiety was that he had spent all he had on Shaukat and there was nothing left for the other two. If Shaukat was not prepared to lend a hand in a family where things were tight there would be no way out. He was getting old and could not feel as confident as before.

Shaukat was a grown man now and, of course, his ways would alter. So he was bound to change but that did not mean that the family's peace and order should be sacrificed. Shaukat understood so much and yet he could not grasp this simple truth. If only he could shout at Shaukat like a vulgar, low born person he would feel less burdened, but a slanging match was impossible for him.

He had received respect from strangers but it was his firstborn who had belittled him in the eyes of others. He seemed to have become unnecessary to the family he had set up. The realisation drove him to distraction as if he were a piece of chaff. The son whom he had thought would provide comfort in the continuous struggle for existence was now in revolt against him in word and deed and even begun to find his father's very being contemptible. It was as if Shaukat had waited twenty-five years for his father to grow old and then get his own back for the years of patient obedience. He knew that without Shaukat's co-operation his much loved family would collapse. Yet he no longer wanted his help. It would be better were he to die in poverty and starvation than to see his son's arrogant ways destroying everything.

When he saw Shaukat's stern expression the whole afternoon and his wife creeping about like a dying woman, the father knew that Shaukat had not got the job. The boy's eyes were swollen. Perhaps he had been crying. Though he knew it all, he still asked. 'What happened? Whom did they take?' Shaukat remained silent. What could he say? He had hoped the job would help him escape from home but now there was no way out.

Mother was carrying the winnowing fan* as she walked towards the kitchen. 'Really,' she said to her husband, 'you don't seem to have much sense.'

Shaukat's dreams are dead. He has now become the spectacle to be observed and his father is the spectator. The mother is the curtain between them, touching both, but not being able to move with life's burdens.

Notes

All words and phrases thought to present difficulty have been marked by an asterisk in the text and are explained below.

Appeasement

inner rooms   rooms used by women members of the family where males would not normally enter

Braj or Vraj   the region in what is now the state of Uttar Pradesh in North India where Krishna is supposed to have lived

Krishna   a major Hindu god whose worship is part of Vaishnavism—Krishna being one of the incarnations of the god, Vishnu. In his human form, Krishna's love for the princess Radha has been celebrated in poetry, song, dance and art throughout India

Puja holidays   major Bengali holiday which falls between the months of September and October and is connected with the worship of the goddess Durga, the consort of Shiva

January Night

gave the lie to his name   His name is derived from the Hindi word, *halka,* which means light in weight, whereas Halku, himself is a heavy man.

cowdung cake   dried cowdung made into flat cakes and used as a cheap fuel in villages throughout the subcontinent

Tarini the Boatman

Ambubachi   a local festival of Bengal

Dasahara   a regional festival to honour the river Ganges

The New Constitution

Akbar Badshah   the greatest of the Mughal emperors of India who ruled from 1556–1605

Congresswalas   members of the Indian National Congress, the political organisation that led the country's struggle for independence from British rule

Angrez   English people

Itlywala   an Italian

Rooswala   a Russian

tommy   a colloquial term for a British soldier

Marwari   a Rajasthani from the state of Marwar—frequently used to refer to businessmen from that community who are found all over the subcontinent

Dinu halwai's   literally, 'Dinu the sweet seller's'

Rooswala Badshah   literally the king of Russia but Mangu is probably referring to Stalin

Red Shirt Movement   the freedom movement started in the Northwest Frontier Province against British rule and linked to the Gandhian nationalist struggle

The Leader

Terrorist Movement   the militant branch of the nationalist movement which disclaimed Gandhian non-violence in favour of armed raids and other acts of sabotage against the British *raj*

Shiva's tandav   the cosmic dance of the Hindu god, Shiva, the destroyer of evil

The Jagirdar and his Dog

Jagirdar   a rural aristocrat

Talati   a petty official employed by the local council

Bapu   a term of respect for someone in authority

A Blind Man's Contentment

Kasi   another name for Benares, a holy city of the Hindus

Rameswaram   a holy city for Hindus in the extreme south of India. A devout Hindu is supposed to go on pilgrimages which will take him to the four corners of the country from the heights of the Himalayas to the southernmost point.

pebbles instead of arecanut   While there are many variations in the preparation of paan, the betelnut leaf, the basic ingredients are a dash of lime, a bit of catechu, a sprinkling of aromatic spices and a few slivers of arecanut.

Lajwanti

Lajo   a diminutive of Lajwanti

Miss Mridula Sarabhai   the daughter of a wealthy industrialist who campaigned actively for the rescuing and rehabilitation of abducted women

Rama/Sri Ram Chandra   (otherwise known as Ram or Rama) the king of Ayodhya in Uttar Pradesh who was a reincarnation of the Hindu god, Vishnu. He is the hero of a Sanskrit epic, Ramayana, in which he struggles against Ravana, king of Lanka to rescue his wife, Sita.

Ram Rajya   Rama's kingdom

Devi   literally, 'goddess'

The Stench of Kerosene

bride price   In some parts of the country instead of the bride's parents paying a dowry to the groom's family, it is the groom's parents that pay the bride's family.

Compulsions

Id or Eid   a Muslim festival celebrated after Ramadan during which month nothing is to be eaten or drunk from dawn to sunset

A Death in Delhi

Sardarji   a term of respect for a Sikh

Connaught Place   the centre of New Delhi, full of smart shops and restaurants

Baby Deer

Oraon and Munda   tribal peoples found in Bihar

Jamaibabu   Jamai in Bengali means son-in-law. Babu is a term of respect like 'mister'.

Manas Sarovar   a lake in the Himalayas in Tibet

Monsoon

Khoka/Khuki   little boy/little girl

winnowing fan   a curved tray made of bamboo cane in which to
    clean the rice before it is cooked

Glossary

Anna   a small coin of little value

Asharh   in the Indian calendar this corresponds to the months of June–July

baksheesh   tip or small gift of money

bhabhi   an elder brother's wife

Bhangi   one of the lowest castes, formerly called untouchables

biriani   a kind of spiced rice cooked with meat

brahmin   a member of the Hindu priestly caste

burqa   a large cloak which covers the entire body and face of a Muslim woman when she goes out in public

chaddar   cloth wrapped over the upper part of the body like a shawl

charpoy   a wooden bed strung with rope

chillum   a small clay pipe for smoking tobacco

dacoits   armed robbers generally operating in gangs

dada   Bengali word for older brother, sometimes shortened to *da*

dak bungalow   bungalows built in remote country places for the use of visiting government officers

dal   lentil

dervesh   Muslim ascetics or mystics generally belonging to a religious order

dhobi   a washerman

didi   Bengali term for older sister, sometimes shortened to *di*.

dhoti   a length of cloth generally about five metres which is tied round the waist and pleated in a variety of ways. It is worn by Hindu men and boys.

dupatta   a piece of cloth worn over a blouse like a stole

gamcha   Bengali term for head cloth

gram   split peas

halwai   a man who makes and sells sweets

henna-tinted   a natural reddish-coloured dye

hookah   a bubble pipe used to smoke tobacco

ilish/hilsa   a fish used in Bengali cuisine

Jumma   Urdu word for Friday

kanji   a rice gruel

koel   an Indian bird similar to the cuckoo

lac-tinted   a kind of resin used as a varnish or nail polish

lakh   100,000

lassi   a popular Punjabi drink made with yoghourt

lat sahibs   a Hindustani corruption of 'lord sahibs' used too describe Englishmen or upper-class Indians

lathi   a long stick used by the police as a weapon

lotus   a kind of water lily

luddi   a folk dance of the Punjab

mahashay   a Bengali term of respect like 'sir'

mahia   a village song of the Punjab

mathali   a wicker hat worn by peasants in West and East Bengal

paan   a green heart-shaped leaf filled with crushed spices chewed after a meal

pachedi   a head cloth

paise/pice   coins like pennies introduced when the currency was decimalised in 1957

Panchatantra   a collection of fables in Sanskirt supposed to have been used by a wise Brahmin teacher to impart moral education to a king's sons

papars/papadams   crisp flat savoury pancakes made of lentil flour

paratha   a type of fried bread

pariahs   the name of a particular caste of untouchables, also a term for stray dogs

peon   government servant such as a postman or clerk

pir   an Urdu word for a holy man who has become a saint

pukka   a Hindi word literally meaning 'ripe' but used to denote something that is genuine or pure

puris   fried bread

purdah   the seclusion of women by keeping them in the house and making them wear some kind of masked garment like a burqa

Quran/Koran   the holy book of Islam

Ramayana   This is one of the great Indian epics, the other being the *Mahabharata*. It is difficult to date as it is the result of many generations of poets and bards reciting it orally. The hero of the *Ramayana* is the brave and just prince Rama who makes an epic journey to rescue his wife Sita who has been abducted by Ravana, the evil king of Lanha

rupee   coin roughly equivalent to 5p

sadhu   a Hindu holy man, often a recluse

sahib bahadur   literally 'valiant sir' in Urdu but generally used sarcastically for someone who struts around like a sahib

shalwar   the baggy trousers worn by men and women in the Punjab and further north. Women wear them with a matching blouse and stole called kurta and dupatta

sari   a woven length of material about six metres in length draped over the body with one end hung over the shoulder. It is the commonest dress for women in most parts of the subcontinent though worn in a variety of ways.

seth   term for a Hindu business man

sheeshum   a tree whose wood is used to make good quality furniture

Sravan   fourth month in the Hindu calendar corresponding to July–August

surma   a kind of mascara

tal   the fruit of the toddy palm whose juice is distilled to make a potent alcoholic drink

tandav   originally the cosmic dance of destruction by Siva, one of the three supreme gods of Hinduism—now taken to mean any kind of wild dance

tandoors   clay ovens popular in the Punjab and the Frontier for roasting meat, now widely used in Indian restaurants specialising in tandoori dishes

tauba! an Urdu exclamation expressing shock. Literally, it is a call to repent

tonga   a two wheeled horse–drawn carriage which can seat three or four passengers

ustad   Urdu word for maestro or expert

Vedas   early religious writings of the ancient Hindus. Written in Sanskrit, they include a collection of songs in praise of the gods (the *Rigveda*), a compilation of magical formulae (the *Atharvaveda*), and chants and prayers for singing during religious ceremonies (the *Samaveda*). There is some doubt as to the dating of the *Vedas*. Some authorities claim it was written in the period around 2500 B.C., others claim it dates from 700 B.C.